NORTH'S POLE

by
LETA BLAKE

An Original Publication from Leta Blake Books

North's Pole by Leta Blake
Cover by Dar Albert
Formatted by BB eBooks

Print Edition

First Print Edition, 2022
ISBN: 9781626226562

Other Books by Leta Blake

Contemporary

Will & Patrick Wake Up Married
Will & Patrick's Endless Honeymoon
Cowboy Seeks Husband
The Difference Between
Bring on Forever
Stay Lucky

Sports

The River Leith

The Training Season Series
Training Season
Training Complex

Musicians

Smoky Mountain Dreams
Vespertine

New Adult

Punching the V-Card

'90s Coming of Age Series
Pictures of You
You Are Not Me

Winter Holidays

North's Pole

Audiobooks

Leta Blake at Audible

Discover more about the author online

Leta Blake
letablake.com

Gay Romance Newsletter

Leta's newsletter will keep you up to date on her latest releases, sales and deals, future writing plans, and more from the world of M/M romance. Join Leta's mailing list today.

Leta Blake on Patreon

Become part of Leta Blake's Patreon community to support her indie publishing expenses and to access exclusive content, deleted scenes, extras, and interviews.

Acknowledgments

Thank you to the following people:

Brian and Cecily

Mom & Dad

The wonderful members of my Patreon who inspire, support, and advise me, especially Susan Buttons and Randall Jussaume

Amy and Kelly for their beta reading and excellent suggestions

Willow and Devon for proofing

Sue Laybourn and Stacey A. for developmental and copy edits

And, most especially, **all my readers** who always make the blood, sweat, and tears of writing worthwhile.

CHAPTER ONE
North

December 21

I T WASN'T LIKE I'd *wanted* to show the entire fucking world my "engorged cock," as the angry mob on Twitter kept calling it. I hadn't meant for *anyone* to see it except for HungryTop34, and I'd only shown *him* because we'd sexted a few times before, and this time he'd begged to see "the whole package."

Maybe it wasn't smart of me (you think?), but I'd sent a picture of my "package." A great shot of it, too. It took twenty minutes just to get the right angle. For his eyes only!

Or so I'd thought.

Because somehow? What I actually did? Was share the photo to my Instagram story, which automatically cross-posted to my Twitter, Facebook, and Snapchat. How had I made such an idiotic mistake? Had I really been that horny and excited I'd gotten confused between the chat on my hookup app and my Insta story?

All signs pointed to yes.

There I was, leaning back in bed, hand around my dick, waiting to hear what HungryTop34 thought of my "package," when my phone began pinging wildly with messages from every social media app I had and with incoming texts from everyone I knew.

Blinking at comments like, "*Ew, bro wtf,*" I sat in stunned confusion until someone commented, "*That's your dick?!?*"

That was when I'd felt it. Just the way everyone described.

My blood turned cold, and my stomach dropped with a horrifying swoop. Vomit surged up my throat, and I feared I was about to heave all over my bed. Luckily, I made it to the bathroom first.

Once I stopped puking and got my brain together enough to figure out I should do something about my massive, enormous, *horrible* error, my hands were shaking so badly I couldn't get the pictures deleted fast enough. I tried. I really did try.

But it was far too late.

Afterward, my mind went blank, like someone had painted it over with that bumpy ceiling spackle they have in old buildings, or maybe it was more like a snowstorm. Just raging, howling, whiteness. Along with an urgent need to escape—to *hide*.

I shoved some stuff into my backpack—left empty on the floor of my closet ever since I quit college last month—and took the stairs two at a time down to the parking garage. I climbed into my favorite Lexus and hightailed it out of Seattle, my home for the last two years.

At first, I didn't know what to do or where to go. I drove blindly onto I-90, fighting traffic and panic. My phone was going bonkers. I dumped it into the central storage compartment beneath the arm rest and blared music so I couldn't hear it vibrating.

As I drove into the darkness, my mind whirled with visions of the never-ending humiliation ahead.

Unfortunately, accidentally uploading a dick pic wasn't my first brush with scandal. Being the child of famous people and standing to inherit millions and millions of dollars, people cared way more than they otherwise would about every little thing I said, did, thought, wore, read, watched, or listened to.

The scrutiny—that's a word my ex-bodyguard Liam had used to describe my situation—was as intense as it was endless.

Gossip sites and tabloids were relentless in their pursuit of information about my family. They stalked not only our social media accounts but also the accounts of our friends. And even people we *weren't* friends with if they thought there was even a chance they knew us. I was convinced there were tabloid reporters following the social media posts of my Seattle apartment's neighbors, hoping to get a glimpse of me in the background of one of their on-site pool or gym pics.

My worst past scandal took place just a few months ago, and it still wasn't dead and buried. It hadn't even been my fault, but I'd taken all the blame.

The situation: I was at a Halloween party thrown by my then-friend Lily Maynard. (Daughter of Eddie Maynard of Farm Fresh Frozen Foodies fame, aka "new money girl" as my Grandmother Astor called her.) I'd had my space alien costume made just for the event, complete with a big, round, gray headpiece, glittery antennae, and gray bodysuit.

I'd always been a big fan of anything extraterrestrial. And dragons! I loved reading stories about these fantasy creatures, watching TV and movies including them, and I loved to draw them. Particularly dragons. Drawing was probably what I was best at in life.

Later, after the scandal blew up, I often wondered: had I dressed as a dragon that night, would things have gone differently? Because of...what was it called? My sister Southerland had told me about it...

Ah, the Butterfly Effect. Change one thing in the past, and you change everything in the present.

But there I was, standing near the chips and salsa, stuffing my face, and obsessing over the fact our college's it-boy, Robson Reynolds, was also at the party. When I'd first arrived, he'd grabbed my ass and whispered in my ear, "Hot aliens come first."

That was a flirty request for sex, wasn't it?

Confused, worried, and hopeful—and kind of turned on—I'd wished I had an NDA handy for him to sign, just in case...

Yeah. An NDA.

Because I *was* "North Astor-Ford of the Astor-Ford hotel/acting fortune," as the gossip sites called me, and I couldn't jump into bed with just anyone. There was too much to consider.

What if the person I had sex with took secret pictures or videos of us and sold them? What if they wrote a thinly veiled blog post or Twitter thread about me and published the details of our encounter for the world's amusement and judgment? What if a girl claimed I got her pregnant? What if I *did* get her pregnant? What if a guy or girl said I gave them an STD? What if they gave *me* an STD? What if they tried to blackmail me for money? What if, what if, *what if?*

Not that I'd been smart enough to consider all the potential consequences on my own. Foresight wasn't one of my gifts, though I had many others, as Grandma Ford always said. She just meant my looks. I couldn't think of anything else I was exceptional at. Well, except for drawing cool aliens and dragons.

But because I wasn't very good at being able to predict what the outcome of any given situation or choice might be, my family had taken extra precautions. Which was why, ever since Southerland and I became teens, our parents had arranged for us and our bodyguards/managers to attend monthly meetings with "image consultants" and family lawyers to check we were staying on track.

My folks always wanted to make sure we understood the potential problems of making a "relationship mistake." Warner Jackson, my dad's manager, once said to me, "A thing which starts out small when it's just you and the girl alone in a room together—a kiss, a hand job, a whispered secret—can escalate into something enormous once it's out in the wider world. Don't ever forget it."

Well, Warner Jackson? I thought as I steered my way toward the mountains. *Ever since I hit send on the message to HungryTop34, I've thought of nothing else.*

Sending that pic had seemed like such a small thing—not my

dick, it was plenty big—but the actual sending of the picture had seemed harmless enough. It'd been a private moment just between HungryTop34 and me. Intimate. Secret.

But now, because of my stupid mistake, it would spiral into a mammoth, huge, thunderous, monstrous, ever-growing, utterly humiliating disastrous crisis which would probably consume my whole life. Maybe it already had, given the state of my phone.

The armrest vibrated insistently with new notifications. I turned the music up again and clutched the steering wheel with both hands. Sweat rolled down my temples, and my stomach lurched, but I kept on driving.

God, how had this happened? The mess was all the app makers' fault!

It shouldn't have been *possible* for a person to set up all that automatic cross-posting! What a terrible idea! When I'd originally chosen the option, I'd felt smart, thinking of the time and effort I'd save myself from then on. But how had I not predicted an accident like this? It was destined to happen.

Stupid app designers! My dad should sue them. No! I realized *I* should! Because I was an adult, and I could do things like that. Yes, I could sue them for a bazillion dollars, which would barely even begin to cover the emotional trauma and damage to my reputation.

Though I couldn't say I had much of a rep left to protect.

Which brought me back to the big scandal at Halloween, the one that'd prompted me to drop out of school: Robson Reynolds had entered the kitchen where I was choking down chips and salsa, sauntered up to me, rested his forearms on my shoulders, grinned, and darted forward to lick a bit of salsa from the corner of my mouth.

Pulling back, he'd given me a wicked smirk. "Getting messy without me, alien?"

I was so *excited* by this hot guy who'd apparently set his sights on me, I didn't even notice all the phones out, all the pictures and videos being taken.

Worse, I didn't look at Robson Reynolds's costume.

I was caught up in his wide shoulders, his piercing blue eyes, his smug smile, and his arms around my neck, dragging me in for what became my first and only kiss with a guy; I was nearly numb with shock.

I'd kissed a number of girls before, usually at parties, in dark closets with the door closed, and I'd touched several sets of breasts, but I'd never been crushed up against another guy's strength before. It sent my head swimming, my senses reeling, and my dick throbbing.

Breaking the kiss, Robson cupped my crotch and announced loudly, "Looks like he likes it both ways." He'd swung around to the room at large, shouting, "Pay up!"

Money passed hands. Robson laughed as he collected it, tucking the green bills into the breast of his costume—at that point, I'd recognized it as a military jacket—and sauntered out of the room without looking back. Feeling like I'd been backhanded, I stared after him, slack-jawed and embarrassed. The cackling teasing of my so-called friends filled my ears. I couldn't get out of there fast enough.

On the elevator down to the ground floor of Lily's apartment building, my phone started buzzing away in my alien costume's side pocket. I knew what that meant: I'd kissed another guy in public, and now the whole world knew about it.

As soon as I reached the parking garage, I drove straight home to my apartment, ignoring my phone as it continued to blow up.

Just the way I was ignoring it now.

That willful ignorance of the fallout of Robson's lips on mine hadn't lasted long. My parents had arrived the next morning with their most terrifying attorney, Lu Weinstein, and I'd had to issue a formal, recorded apology for my "mistake."

Because somehow, someway, it was *my* fault Robson Reynolds was wearing a Nazi armband on his military costume that night (what a disgusting asshole!), and it was *my* fault he'd kissed me in the kitchen, and it was *my* fault people had posted videos and pictures of it all over the internet.

North Astor-Ford's new boyfriend is beyond problematic, and here's why...

North Astor-Ford's out of the closet and into the foulest of messes...

North Astor-Ford licked by Neo-Nazi and likes it...

North Astor-Ford—

It'd gone on and on.

And I'd done what was asked of me.

I'd apologized for Robson's offensive costume and for kissing him while he wore it—though I'd actually had nothing to do with his choice to wear such a horrific get-up, and I hadn't kissed him at all; he'd kissed *me!*

And the family attorneys made sure I apologized for *attending* the party and apologized for embarrassing my family, and for being gay (even though I'm not? I'm bisexual! And even if I were gay, there's nothing *wrong* with that!), and finally, I apologized for basically *existing*.

Meanwhile, Lily posted a tearful video on her social media saying Robson, and I had ruined her party, and she'd never forgive him or me for it. So long to those six whole weeks of friendship! The longest one of my short life. Unless you counted my kinda-sorta friendship with Liam, and Southerland said I couldn't count that because he was my employee.

Robson himself made a stilted, subdued apology for the costume after being kicked off the university basketball team. He'd said: "I'm also sorry I ever met North Astor-Ford. He's led me to make poor choices. I'm going to distance myself from him and do some hard thinking. I'm going to be a better man from now on."

Like it was my fault? Like we were even friends, or boyfriends, or more than casual acquaintances before that night? Like *I* picked his costume?

After the Robson incident, I became a pariah on campus, more for ruining Robson's potential basketball career and for upsetting Lily Maynard—that innocent pretty princess of a girl—than for being an idiot who'd dressed as an alien for Halloween and somehow been caught up in a prank kiss from an asshole who'd just wanted to drag me into his nasty game and sully my reputation.

Sully. That was a good, fancy word. My folks' attorney used it a lot when talking about how careful Southerland and I needed to be in our behavior.

To this day, no one has ever asked me how I felt about the kiss. No one cared how it'd affected *me* as a person or that I'd felt violated and sick that my first kiss with a guy had been stolen by such a horrible human being. No one had *ever* asked if I was all right or not.

Liam would have, but he wasn't around anymore.

Because I'd fired him.

Memory aching, I gripped the steering wheel, maneuvering around trucks, and wondering how many of the drivers knew about my scandal with Robson and now how many had seen my dick.

Eventually, I realized I couldn't drive forever. It was getting late, and I was shaky with nerves and exhaustion. I needed to choose a place as a destination, but there was nowhere on earth I wanted to be. Except with Liam. I'd be safe if I were next to him.

I knew where he was living these days. At his mom's house. In Idaho.

But that was hours and hours away, and I couldn't just go there. What would his mom think? If her son's former protectee showed up in the middle of the night wanting comfort after posting his dick pic for all the world to see? That'd be rude. And an Astor was never rude in public, and a Ford was never rude at all, so I had to be polite for sure. My bloodlines were counting on it.

My panic had turned to a buzzy itch beneath my skin, and as I struggled to think of where to hide out, my mind offered up one of my last memories of Liam from three Decembers ago.

"I worked at the chalet all through high school," he'd said, his voice warm and steady, brimming with nostalgia. *"It was like a second home to me."*

"Did you need a second home?" I'd asked.

He'd smiled, shiny as a penny with all that rich, red hair and his sparkling, cinnamon-brown eyes. *"Don't we all need as many places to call 'home' as we can get?"*

Shaking the memory from my head, my car's lights cutting out a path on the dark road, I said out loud, "I just want any kind of home right now. Anywhere to feel safe."

An idea came to me. What if, instead of trying to get to Liam at his mom's place, I went to the chalet where he'd once worked instead? I could stay there through Christmas Day, avoid the world and my parents, and maybe I'd get the guts to seek out Liam before I left... Apologize to him for firing him like that.

I wracked my brain for the name of the place. I remembered it rhymed, but I couldn't quite grab hold of the details. I'd just given up when it came to me.

Camp Bay Chalet.

I pulled off the road and punched the name of the inn into my GPS.

As I hit enter, the robotic woman's voice announced, *"Starting route to Camp Bay, Idaho."*

I felt safer already.

CHAPTER TWO
Liam

December 22

*North Astor-Ford, son of hotel heiress Susan Astor and actor Deacon Ford, is in piping hot—yes, that's **boiling** hot—water! This time over an, ahem, inappropriate upload to his social media accounts. The internet is burning down over this scorching and raunchy shot!*

"WHY ARE YOU looking at that garbage?" I asked my sister.

"What? TikTok?" Maeve ran her thumb over the screen, navigating away from the video discussing the latest bumble my former protectee, twenty-one-year-old North Astor-Ford, had made.

She reclined on the sofa, propping up her swollen feet after a shift on the ER's hard floors and scrolling TikTok like her life depended on it. "Your 'garbage' is my 'yummy treat.'"

"It's shameless gossip about a guy who—" I stopped myself.

Maeve glanced up, one perfectly shaped, black brow lifting, as her lips twisted into that annoying smirk, which, as her twin, I was all too familiar with. I'm pretty sure she'd smirked at me like that in the womb.

"It's also cat-in-Santa-hat videos and old people dancing and puppies in the rain and babies tasting sour things for the first time and KPop idols and holiday memes and—"

"Stop. I get it."

"Clearly, you don't."

"Maybe *you're* the one who doesn't get it."

Immature and ineffective as a come-back goes, sure, but it was all I had in me when my mind kept circling back to the implications of that TikTok about North.

I gave myself a stern, internal lecture.

You have no right to give a damn anymore when it comes to North Astor-Ford and his sexy problems.

Avoidance had worked in the past, and I could make it work again. I turned my focus to helping my four-year-old nephew put all his Tonka Trucks, Matchbox Cars, and Paw Patrol figures back in the big, blue bin they belonged in. We crawled around on the floor together as Aiden sang the "clean up" song I'd taught him.

Aiden was an adorable kid—red hair and gingerbread-brown eyes like mine. It was my main job to take care of him and his little brother Jack. Everyone said Aiden looked just like me, and it was true. He didn't have my freckles yet, but I figured a few more years of playing outside in the sun would do the trick.

Jack, currently down for a nap, was eighteen months old and cuter than a basketful of puppies, but he looked like his father—aka the bastard who'd left them—with his light brown hair and sparkling blue eyes.

Saying it was my job to watch them was an inaccurate way to put it. I wasn't *paid* to do it. Not exactly. In exchange for providing childcare while Mom worked at her accounting job and Maeve worked at the hospital, I received free room and board at my mom's house. I only had to watch the kids for three days since Mom was mostly retired, which left me with time to do the occasional gig work as a rent-a-cop at the local ski resorts.

I'd also taken up selling free-lance excursions around Lake Pend Oreille for tourists via enterprising travel apps. It wasn't bad money during the peak tourism months. But I hadn't had steady bodyguard work since North.

I hadn't even looked for any.

"Give me that," I said, crawling over to Maeve and surrendering to my curiosity.

Grabbing the phone from her hand, I accidentally cued the next video. It showed a man stumbling into a garbage can, knocking it over, tripping, and falling down a hill, all while a whiny, sing-songy voice crooned "oh no" over and over in the background. What entertainment people gleaned from this app was beyond me, but it didn't matter. I needed to know about North, even if he wasn't my business anymore and hadn't been in three years.

"How do I...?" I tried swiping up and down, but that just brought me to a video of dancing teenage girls in Sexy Santa get-ups with half-exposed chests, followed by a video of a black cat eating a holiday-themed treat with a superior expression on his face while a male voiceover narrated the cat's smug inner-thoughts. "Christ, get that video back, will you?" I thrust the phone back to her.

"Yeah, *Christ*, Mama," Aiden echoed. "Get the bideo back."

"I've told you not to teach him to take God's name in vain," Maeve scolded. "Mom will have a heart attack."

"He didn't take God's name—"

"He did, Liam."

"He took His Son's name in vain." Shockingly, she didn't fry me with her glare. "Never mind. Just find that video again."

"Brat." She frowned at the phone as she scrolled. "I don't know why you still care about that spoiled kid. He left you jobless during a pandemic in the middle of a crap economy. You owe him nothing."

"I know."

It was true, but it wasn't the whole story.

I'd never told Maeve the truth about North and why he'd let me go during his senior year of high school. Having a bodyguard, even a nineteen-year-old one like I'd been back then, was always going to be a pain in North's ass. But having a bodyguard he was attracted to was oh-so-much worse.

I couldn't blame North for wanting to put himself out of his misery by putting *me* as far away as possible. The fact it'd helped me out of my misery, too—because the attraction was very much mutual—was something I hadn't shared with anyone in my family. Though something told me Mom and Maeve both suspected the truth.

Maybe I had a bit of a hero complex, too. There was a reason I'd started training to go into the protection business at eighteen, after all. I liked saving the day and being a man someone could depend on. And boy, oh boy, did North need someone to depend on.

In addition to all his scrapes and messes, he'd been held back in school two different times, making him a sixteen-year-old freshman when we'd met, and, when I left, an eighteen-year-old senior. The same age I'd been when I started working for his family.

He'd just barely managed to stay a full year ahead of his younger sister, so he didn't face the embarrassment of sharing the same classes as her at their boarding school.

I believed my attraction to North said way more about *me* than it did about him and some of what it said I didn't enjoy confronting. Which was why I'd been planning to quit at the beginning of the winter break. I'd wanted to give his family time to find a new bodyguard before the next semester of school began and for me to hopefully find a new job elsewhere.

But even if I hadn't been able to find work—and I hadn't—I knew while our age gap was small (only three years), the situation was still inappropriate. Having feelings for one's protectee was never a good look for many reasons.

North hadn't waited for the break to fire me. He'd done it at

Thanksgiving. Quick, without warning. Two weeks' severance. I still believed it'd been good he let me go when he did, even if it had stung in its suddenness and even if the timing *had* meant moving back in with my mom.

"Here," Maeve said, passing the phone over before heaving herself upright. She patted the sofa next to her. "I want to watch too."

I supposed if the whole world were talking about North again, it would only be a matter of time until Maeve and everyone with an internet connection heard the details. I did as she asked, settling in beside her.

Aiden kept putting his toys away. He was such a good kid. Jack would have started to take them back out without my direct supervision. Of course, he was just a baby. I shouldn't have expected too much from him.

Aiden kept on humming to himself as I rubbed a sweaty palm over my knee, nervous about what North might have uploaded to his social media accounts that could cause such a huge outcry. I had my suspicions—

And they were proven correct in short order.

The TikTok-er was a young brunette woman with hair that was half-long, half-short, but not really a mullet either. She wore enormous peppermint candy-shaped earrings and very long fingernails which were painted with sparkling candy-cane stripes. She seemed more gleeful than outraged as she described North's mishap.

And it truly seemed like a mishap to me.

Though some on the internet were apparently calling it a gross violation of human decency, and others were saying it was sexual harassment via non-consensual worldwide web exposure.

"It's true I never consented to see that pic," the woman said, eyes wide with delight. "But it's not like I'm mad about it!" She laughed. "If you're going to upload your tool to the bona fide inter-damn-net in this year of our Lord twenty-twenty-two, at least make sure you're showing off a nice hammer, am I right? And, oh my God, North Astor-Ford has one *divine* hammer!" The TikTok-er pretended to gag on a dick before adding, "Just call him Thor! Whew, what a dick pic!"

"Good lord," Maeve murmured.

"What was that about taking the Lord's name?" I asked under my breath.

"Dick pic!" Aiden sang cheerfully, making a song of it as he put the last of his Tonka trucks away. "Dicky-dick pic, dick pic, dickidy pic."

"Great." Maeve passed her phone to me, rising to go heft Liam up onto her hip. "Honey, you can't say that. It's not nice."

"Dick pic?"

"Yes."

"Why?"

"Oh, man." She rubbed her forehead. "I'm too tired for this."

"Need to refuel, Mama?" Aiden asked, his little eyebrows scrunching with worry. "Is it time for a snack?"

Maeve kissed his chubby cheek. "Yeah. Let's go see what we can eat." She turned to me, reaching for her phone. "Don't get too wrapped up in this. He's not your problem. Just remember that."

I nodded as she took Aiden into the kitchen.

Not my protectee. Not my problem.

I sat in silence, contemplating the wood floors and the patterned carpet where Jack liked to toddle and Aiden liked to push his toy cars around and create imaginary lands for his Paw Patrol figures.

I changed my focus to the wide window opposite the sofa and the view of Mr. McNally's yard with his various Christmastime-only garden gnomes and newly added glow-in-the-dark Nativity scene.

Taking a long breath, I mentally repeated the mantra: *Not my problem.* So why did North still *feel* like my problem?

I tried the technique a psychologist who'd signed up for one of my tours of Pend Oreille had talked about as a good method for dealing with anxiety. Centering myself in what I could see, feel, smell, and touch, I scanned the living room of the house I grew up in, noting the way things had changed and the way they'd stayed the same.

The couch beneath my butt was different from the one Maeve and I jumped on playing *the floor is lava.* This one was way more comfortable and purchased after Dad's death eight years ago—a navy sectional which accommodated more family members at once.

The wooden rocking chair in the corner was the same as ever, though the seat pillow was different, having been replaced by Mom after Jack scribbled all over the old one with a Sharpie.

The flatscreen was, of course, much bigger than the one I'd grown up watching, but it still played Mom's recorded "stories" every night, just like when I was a kid. And it flickered a muted cartoon right now.

Not my problem. North is not my problem.

We'd put up a real Christmas tree just last weekend, and the kids had had a blast helping to decorate it. No more fake plastic trees like Dad had insisted on when we were growing up. He'd always claimed cleaning up the needles just wasn't worth the heavenly evergreen scent.

Another deep breath in and out. The smell of pine was, to me, entirely worth any cleanup necessary. Besides, hand vacs were basically invented for just that reason.

The stockings on the mantel were new, too, Mom having accidentally thrown away the box containing the ones from Maeve's and my childhood while she was cleaning out the garage two years ago. But the new ones were bright and cheerful, with our names sewn on in sequins, and the boys loved them. Over the last few years, I'd grown to love them, too.

Everything in my mom's house was comfortable, cozy, and entirely the opposite of life in the Astor-Ford mansion in Los Angeles. That place wasn't a home. It was a beautiful, chaotic prison.

At least, that was how it'd felt to me, and it was how it'd seemed to feel to North back when I was his manager/bodyguard. Back when I'd off-and-on lived with him there.

I remembered all too well the second—and last—Christmas I'd spent in the Astor-Ford mansion. What a peculiar, foreign day that'd been. North's parents had been as full of liquor as the house had been full of intimate strangers. No familial sense to the holiday at all.

Plus, Victoria Astor, North's maternal grandmother, was always in top sniping form over the holidays. Full of sharp comments about the decorations, the canapes, the music, as well as subtle *and* overt digs towards North's parents, his other grandmother Mrs. Ford, his sister Southerland, and even North himself.

I could only imagine what Christmas was going to be like for North now. Going home for the holidays to that bitter, critical grandmother and to those drunken, semi-negligent parents had always been hard, but it was guaranteed to be extra rough with this new scandal hanging over his head.

If only he hadn't fired his last manager/bodyguard, Eleesha, on the day he turned twenty-one. She would have kept him out of this mess.

Shortly after he'd let her go, Eleesha had reached out to me with a text: *Sorry, Liam. I tried my best, but he's determined to stand on his own two feet. If only he had the brains to know where his damn feet are!*

Maybe that was unkind of her, but it was also true.

North was any number of wonderful, notable things: kind, gentle, funny (usually inadvertently), a good sport, ungodly handsome, wealthy beyond most folks' wildest dreams, pampered, privileged, sweet, gentle, and did I mention his looks? Gorgeous, *gorgeous* kid.

But I had to admit he'd always been a little lacking in intellectual strengths.

Okay, that *was* unkind.

But it was a damn good thing North had all those other qualities because he certainly wasn't going to be *thinking* his way into any great positions in life.

Don't get me wrong, I adored the kid far beyond what was professional or right—which was why it'd been a good thing he'd fired me—but a genius he was not.

Apparently, a guy didn't need to wear smarty-pants for me to be attracted to or fall in love with him. All he really needed to possess was a good heart. And North's heart was good in abundance.

That face didn't hurt, either.

Nor did his nicely muscled body.

Or his eternal trying-so-hard-but-failing plights.

Not that I'd ever been in *love* with him. Not at all.

With Maeve and Aiden safely out of the room, I got on my own phone and hunted up the currently trending hashtags on Twitter, looking for more information about how this mishap occurred. Had North made an official statement and apology yet? And if not, why?

I rolled my eyes at the highest trending hashtag for the scandal, #NorthsPole, and was horrified to find the dick pic itself was still floating around in the ether, easily searchable, even nearly eleven hours after the event.

The saying was true: the internet *was* forever. From now on, someone would always be able to take an unapproved gander at North's dick. Poor kid. He had to be humiliated.

Not that he had much to be humiliated about. Damn, his piece was a doozy.

Perve, my brain chastised.

Hey, I didn't try to see it on purpose! I defended.

North's pole was out there everywhere, and a simple scroll of the hashtag had it landing on my phone screen again and again. There was only so much squinting and denial I could engage in before I had to admit to myself I'd definitely seen North's dick now. Not in the way I'd fantasized about in the months before (and following) my firing, but in an entirely different, nonconsensual context that made me feel icky inside.

Closing the app, I leaned back and sighed, staring out at the grungy, leftover snow from last week's storm, and at the flat, overcast sky outside. It was unseasonably warm today. Almost forty degrees. Unheard of this time of year. Christmas in these parts wasn't always white and wonderful, but it was always *cold*.

My mind went back to another day of unseasonable holiday weather and the first time I ever saw North's face.

"It still says forty degrees!" Susan Astor exclaimed, pausing our interview yet again to look at the weather app on her phone.

Shoving the sides of her brunette bob behind her ears, she rose from the sofa, stepped past her handsome actor husband, Deacon Ford's legs, and peered at the sun sparkling on the pool. The blue rectangle was clearly visible from the living room's huge, movable wall of windows.

Currently, the pool deck was festooned with poinsettias, Christmas roses, and bustling servants laying tablecloths, fine Christmas-themed china, and silverware on several long tables flanked by silk-covered chairs and a flower arch garlanded with twinkle lights.

"In December?" Mr. Ford chuckled, winking at me before casting his eye quickly around to make sure Lu Weinstein, his attorney, and Eddie Monroe, my boss, were also charmed by his cute reply. "Surely

not, my love. It's LA, not Iceland."

Eddie laughed, and Lu cracked a smile for the first time since he'd led us into the room for the interview. Which hadn't happened yet since Ms. Astor couldn't stay seated long enough to participate, and yet refused to let it happen without her.

"Just let me tell them about the new flowers I've requested to replace those hideous gardenias in the flower arch. I'll be right back. I hate to waste your time, but this is urgent."

During her absence, Mr. Ford behaved as if we were there to see him as fans. He paraded out story after story of on-set shenanigans and "hilarious" tales of excess that made my cheeks heat with embarrassment for him.

After Ms. Astor returned, we'd just barely gotten started with the interview again when her panic about the weather returned.

"The forecast claims it's going to be like this all day," she fretted, poking at her phone like it might change its mind if she checked again. "This party will be a disaster. We'll have to move everything inside, Deacon. Which means we'll need to clear out the upstairs function room and reset everything before evening, and I just don't—"

Eddie cleared his throat. "Mr. Ford, Ms. Astor, we'll be happy to return on a better day."

North's parents exchanged glances, and I thought we were about to be dismissed. But Mr. Ford's eyebrows moved all over the place in some silent communication, and Ms. Astor's shoulders sank. She peered outside again with despair, murmuring, "Maybe Andy can get some attractive outdoor heaters in place before the guests arrive?"

"I'm certain he can," Mr. Ford said comfortingly, reaching for her hand to kiss her fingertips. "There. That fixes it, doesn't it?"

Fussing for only a moment more, Ms. Astor finally turned her attention to me. "Well, you're certainly handsome enough for the job."

I blinked, and Eddie clapped me on the shoulder, saying, "I brought the handsomest and youngest-looking one, just like you asked."

I was confused. What did my looks have to do with this interview? I thought they were looking for protection for their son while he was away at school.

"He definitely looks young enough to pass," Mr. Ford said, scrutinizing me. "He's good, you say? Responsible? Mature?"

"Of course. One of the best I've got right now," Eddie confirmed. "He's not just a pretty face."

"And he's how old?"

"Nineteen. Recently graduated. But I assure you, he's highly skilled."

"I'm sorry," I interrupted. I might've been young, and I might've looked even younger, but I didn't like the feeling the interview was giving me. They were talking about me as if I were the product being bartered for, not just my skills and labor. "What do my age and appearance have to do with protecting your son?"

"Oh, well, he can't go to school with someone ugly or old, can he? It would draw unpleasant attention to him. It's better, at his age, to have protection that blends in," Ms. Astor explained, glancing at her husband for support.

Mr. Ford swirled his drink, re-crossed his legs, and said, "North tends to find himself in scrapes; most aren't of his own making, but he has poor judgment in friends, and he's…how should I put this?"

The baton was passed back to Ms. Astor. "He's an adorable, lovable young man, but he isn't the sharpest crayon in the box." She smiled conspiratorially. "He needs more help than just keeping him clear of the paparazzi. We're looking for someone who can protect not only his body but his reputation as well. Are you up for a job like that?"

I frowned. I'd expected straightforward work, and their offer felt tainted somehow.

"Oh, wait a moment! There's Andy now," Ms. Astor said, leaping up and nodding to a tall, stiff-legged man who'd come outside to check on the progress for the party. "Come with me, Deacon. You know he *only respects you."*

"We should fire him and replace him with someone who respects you," Mr. Ford said, frowning and rising to his feet.

"No, we can't do that. He's the best, and I only want the best for my parties."

Excusing themselves again, they disappeared, heading outside to deal with the ongoing weather and party crisis.

Eddie turned to me. "This is a good gig. They pay very well. It'll look fantastic on your resume. You'd be a fool not to take it."

"The kid's sweet, and you'll like him," Lu added.

"I'd prefer to meet the proposed protectee before I agree." I tried to keep my phrasing professional. I might have been young, but I wasn't going to be taken on a ride or let them think I didn't deserve respectful treatment.

"That shouldn't be a problem," Lu said, rising. "Let me see if we can find him."

Once it was just the two of us, Eddie stood, gripped my shoulder, and whispered, "Be smart about this, Liam. You're not going to find a better first career move." With his usual lack of grace, he added, "I've got to hit the john."

Alone in the room, I stared out at the sparkling pool and breathed in the perfumed air of the Astor-Ford's living room—a signature scent Ms. Astor had declared when Eddie had commented on it—until I grew bored of watching the animated conversation taking place between the Astor-Fords and their party planner.

I crossed the room, passing the baby grand, to check out the view from the other wall of moveable windows.

There, in the greenish-brown of the sun-bleached backyard, a young man stood. He wore a black and white Christmas sweater over jeans, and he looked like he was twenty or twenty-one years old—older than me. But if he were North, as I suspected he must be, I knew he was younger than that. Sixteen, Eddie had said.

But, Christ, he was gorgeous.

Black hair that glistened in the sun, a haze of stubble on his cheeks, and smiling lips that were as pink as California poppies.

A fuzzy, tall dog—a Goldendoodle—came bounding toward him, knocking him over with the ease of a deer crashing into a trashcan. North fell to his ass, laughing and reaching for the happy, bouncing dog. The sweetness of his energy, the sparkle which seemed to light up the air around him, made my breath catch. I stared at him.

And somehow, I knew. This guy? This guy was special.

"I told the Astor-Fords you'd like to meet their son," Lu said from just behind me. I'd been so caught up I hadn't even heard him approach. "Ah, I see you've spotted him already. Handsome kid, isn't he?"

"Not bad," I murmured. "He seems sweet."

"Sweet as pecan pie and dumb as a doorknob."

We both turned around at the return of the Astor-Fords. Ms. Astor's hair was tossed from the wind, and she stewed miserably over the state of her party. "We've sent an employee out looking for North, Mr..." She trailed off. "Uh, I'm sorry; what was your name again?"

"Liam Kelly." The ease with which these people trusted me to look after their son, to be the protector of both his body and mind, trusting the word of Eddie and requiring little other information struck me as careless. If I turned down the work, who knew what sort of man they might hire without making the proper inquiries?

"Well, Liam, we have someone looking for him now."

"Never mind. I don't need to meet him," I said, palms going clammy with the sense I was choosing something fateful. "I'll take the job."

"Oh, good," Mr. Ford said with evident relief. "Let's sign the contracts and be done with it all." He motioned at Lu Weinstein's stack of papers, resting this whole time on the coffee table.

I took one last glance out the window. North threw a squeaky Rudolph toy for his dog and laughed in delight as the animal fetched it back to him.

I sat down, took up the pen, and signed the papers.

Jerking free of the memory, an ache in my chest for the boy I'd protected and grown to care for, I scanned online for more information on North's current predicament.

There'd been no official statement yet. No carefully crafted apology from North's family's handlers. Because of that, the wolves were out prowling the zeros and ones of cyberspace with knives as teeth, ready to take a hunk of North's flesh. Everyone was too busy imagining the worst intentions from the kid simply because he was rich and gorgeous...

Not that a lot of rich and gorgeous kids *aren't* entitled jerks, but...

Not North.

Not really.

I sighed and did something I hadn't let myself do in many months. I pulled up the Find My iPhone app and checked North's location.

It wasn't my fault North had never revoked my Find My iPhone privileges. Though I suppose it *was* my fault for never suggesting he or Eleesha do so. I guess I hadn't been ready to let him go, and that one last thread of connection kept me feeling close to him.

But it wasn't a sense of closeness that hit me when I saw just where he was. It was a jolt of shock.

"What's he doing there, of all places?" I asked aloud like a lunatic. North was less than thirty minutes away. "Why isn't he at home? It's three days before Christmas."

Things had to be bad if he wasn't in L.A. gearing up for the family's whirlwind of various holiday activities. I was exhausted just remembering the many parties, charity events, galas, and get-togethers the Astor-Fords hosted or attended every year between Christmas and New Year. Worry brewed in my gut, mixed with sour anxiety.

"Oh, North. What are you *doing?*"

He'd fired Eleesha, and if the gossip columns were right, he had no protection these days. He was undoubtedly alone. Or did he have someone with him? A friend? A girlfriend? A *boyfriend?*

No telling.

After only a moment's more hesitation, I did another thing I hadn't allowed myself to do since the day I left. I sent him a text.

Saw what's going on. Seems like a big mess. Need someone to listen? I'm here for you.

Rubbing a hand over my face, I leaned back again. Now there was nothing to do but wait.

Unless…

Unless I wanted to get in my car and drive.

CHAPTER THREE

North

I T'D TAKEN FIVE and a half hours driving through the night over some gnarly parts of the I-90 to reach Camp Bay Chalet.

At about three in the morning, when my eyes started feeling sticky, and I couldn't concentrate anymore, I'd exited at Ritzville and checked in at a place called the Emperor Motel. Let me just say the town was *not* ritzy, and the motel was *not* fit for an emperor or really anyone at all.

But I'd plugged my now-dead phone into the extra battery I stored in the glove compartment, left it behind in the car, and went inside to grab a few hours of rest. I'd woken the next morning around ten to continue my journey.

When I finally arrived at my destination and pulled into a surprisingly crowded parking lot at Camp Bay Chalet, I was exhausted and sick to my stomach.

The place was just like Liam had described: thick logs making an old-fashioned, three-story building. It looked old, *really* old like it'd been built before either of my grandmothers were born.

Covered balconies ran along the outside of the second floor, and they, and the roofed entranceway, were topped in pads of snow and decorated in evergreen garlands. It looked like a gingerbread chalet.

The front door showed off an enormous wreath with a red bow, and over to the side of the house was a tall, live Christmas tree, planted who-knows-when and decorated with big red, gold, and silver ornaments, which flashed and sparkled in the sun.

All around, on the trees and mountains, and on the building itself, snow glistened, with a slushy layer melting on top. I parked in the lot next to a Dodge truck, staring at the chalet, trying to decide what to do next. Would the people working inside recognize me? Had they seen my dick?

I'd just gotten up my nerve to go into the B&B and check in, when the owner—Rhonda? I thought that was what Liam had said her name was—opened the chalet's front door, smiled warmly, and waved me in. Covering my head as best as I could with the hoodie, I obeyed, silently begging whoever and whatever might hear my prayers during this holiday season that she wouldn't recognize my face or name.

Rhonda didn't.

She was everything Liam had described to me—warm, kind, and had a nice smile set into a square jaw. "What can I do for you?"

"A room, please."

Her grin faded. "I'm so sorry. Every year we host a cozy Christmas week for select guests, and we're usually booked a year in advance. If you'd like, I can give you recommendations for another place to stay around Lake Pend Oreille."

Stomach dropping, I wiped a shaky hand over my face, not sure what to do next. It was clear my bad luck had followed me all the way from Seattle. Tears stung my eyes.

Another employee—a man wearing an ugly Christmas sweater and a name tag reading *Sal*—arrived from another room. Unfortunately, *he* recognized my face. I could tell by the way his expression lit up, but he was professional enough not to bring it up at least. I wondered if he'd seen my dick pic. Probably. Though there was a certain twinkle in his eye that made me feel sure he had.

"Oh, Rhonda, wait a moment," Sal said. "We do have availability, after all. Room 11? They can't make it."

"The Jablonskis? Ah. That's too bad." Rhonda frowned.

"Though they'd warned me last month they might not come. His mother is sick. Bad timing."

"Sad for us," Sal said with a smile. "But lucky for the Little Prince here." He took Rhonda's place at the laptop.

"Lucky for sure," Rhonda said, patting my shoulder as she passed me off. "Sal here can get you all set up, Mr. Astor-Ford."

She *had* recognized me! Had *she* also seen my penis? I didn't know for sure, but my cheeks heated up like a bonfire on Christmas Eve.

"Welcome. We're happy to have you here." Still smiling warmly, Rhonda bustled away into what looked like the main dining room for the chalet.

Sal's fingers clacked over the keys, and he nodded firmly when he accomplished what he needed. "Here we are. Room 11. It's not our biggest room, and it doesn't have our best view, but it should do the trick if you're just looking to stay for the night."

"No. For the week," I blurted. *Maybe forever.*

"The week it is," Sal said without hesitation.

As he continued to tap away, I looked around the place.

The interior reception area of the chalet had exposed, warm wood everything—walls, floors, ceiling. There were some nice rugs and cozy couches in front of a fireplace, and a more casual seating area across from the reception desk. Every flat surface was decorated with some kind of greenery or festive ribbons. Twinkle lights decorated the wide logs making up the ceiling. The entire place felt a little tacky and foreign and far, far, *far* away from Seattle—or L.A.

"All booked in." Sal reached out for my credit card. I handed it over, and he didn't even blink at it being a Black American Express. He did, however, say, "I'm sure you hear this all the time, but I'm a big fan of your father's. One time I flew to New York to see him in *After the Sun, the Roses.* I'd hoped to get his autograph, but he didn't come out the stage door after the show."

I gave a tight-lipped smile. What was I supposed to say now? I never knew. My father obviously wasn't here with me, and it wasn't as if I carried cards with his autograph around in my back pocket.

But Sal dropped the subject, starting in on a detailed spiel about all the wonderful activities Camp Bay Chalet had planned for Christmas week. "We know you'll enjoy your holiday here. We pride ourselves on making sure all our guests do."

I hitched my bag up on my shoulder and said, as politely as possible. "Can I have my key please?"

"Of course. Let me help with your luggage or..." He tilted his head, a line creasing the space between his brows. "Or is *that* all you've brought?" He sounded mildly scandalized. It must have looked odd—*the* North Astor-Ford showing up at the last minute during their special Christmas week with nothing more than a Black Card and a backpack.

"This is it."

"I see." Sal cleared his throat, picked up an old-fashioned metal key from a board of them behind the desk, and motioned for me to follow. "Let me take you up to your room. It's right this way."

Four hours later, the vibrating sound coming from the drawer where I'd stuffed my phone was driving me nuts. I should have paid more attention when Southerland tried to teach me how to turn on silent mode. I'd buried it beneath the few pairs of socks and the even-fewer pairs of underwear I'd stuffed into my backpack as I'd left my apartment. But they did nothing to muffle the phone rattling against the wood.

I wished I'd just let the phone die instead of charging it over-night. The incoming messages were constant. Endless. Why couldn't they all just leave me alone?

I pulled a pillow even tighter over my ears, but it didn't block out the sound. Sitting up, holding the pillow still wrapped around my head in desperation, I looked around to see if there was a better place to stuff it. Somewhere with more padding.

There was not.

Unless I wanted to chuck it into the gas fireplace and turn it on.

The room I'd checked into was quaint, with a queen-sized bed taking up so much space it strained the room's ability to hold the rest of the furniture: the antique-looking chest of drawers, a chair by the farthest window, and a small table beneath it.

Plus, a thin, old-fashioned wooden desk sat beside the fireplace with a small matching chair. Over the mantel hung a mirror, and a second, full-length one hung on the back of the door to the adjoining bathroom—which was also quaint, and small, and not a good place to hide a vibrating phone.

The windows looked like they opened...

Maybe I could toss it outside into one of the withering, melty snowbanks.

I *would* have turned it off altogether or let it die, but my parents might think I was dead or kidnapped, and if they weren't actually relieved to be rid of my stupid ass, they might send someone out to look for me. And *that'd* cause all kinds of additional trouble. They might even issue a missing person alert, and I'd be on the news for *two* embarrassing reasons.

At least if my family could see my location on the surveillance apps I knew were installed on my phone, they wouldn't freak out as much.

About me being kidnapped or dead anyway.

They might freak out about *other* things, like the dick pic, why I'd come *here* of all places, or what to do if I never answered my phone to listen to their scolding or never worked with their attorneys to issue the necessary apology. But at least I wouldn't add "gone missing" fears to their already overloaded list of problems due to me.

And, God, those problems felt huge.

"Fuck," I whispered, squeezing my eyes shut and gasping for air. "Why am I so stupid?"

After the Robson incident, I'd tried extra hard to be careful and private. Like, HungryTop34 hadn't even known it was North Astor-Ford he'd been texting with. He'd thought I was a dark-haired little twink named Riley who'd just moved up from San Fran.

I'd even set up my hookup app account with a fake picture I'd gotten from a stock photo site. All the guys I'd messaged with and jerked off with online had no idea I was North Astor-Ford. None at all. I'd been *so* careful.

HungryTop34 didn't know who I was.

Or he *hadn't* known it. It was possible he'd guessed by now he'd been messaging with North Astor-Ford of the Astor-Ford ho-tel/acting fortune, given the timing of the dick pic and the words attached to it.

Here's the whole package. Hungry for it?

Get it? HungryTop? I'd felt very clever.

Fuck.

I was the farthest thing from clever.

It made me sick to think HungryTop34 might be out there giving interviews or posting TikToks about what I'd messaged to him in private before I'd fucked everything up.

I balled up even tighter on the bed, wishing I could block the world out for the rest of my life. Maybe I could. I'd just stay holed up in Camp Bay Chalet until I died or until I finally got the nerve to contact Liam.

So…until I died.

And why *had* I come running to Liam?

Because if he were with me now, I knew he'd make me feel safe, even though the whole world was currently staring at, discussing, dissecting, and commenting on my dick. He'd make me feel cocooned away from all that. He'd tell me it was okay I'd fucked up. He'd say, despite it all, he still liked me.

Maybe even loved me?

I scoffed out loud. Extreme wishful thinking. Besides, I'd kicked him out and couldn't ask him to come back now.

Besides, it wasn't *right* for me to do that, was it?

Especially not when I'd ruined his life by firing him, and all because I'd fallen in love with him and wanted him to hold me down, push my ass cheeks apart, and fuck me.

Before I'd fired Liam, I'd told my sister about my crush because Southerland, despite being three years younger than me, was smart like a whip and good at planning, making strategies, and other complicated stuff. Like algebra.

"I think I'm in love with Liam."

Southerland rolled over on her pillow-strewn bed and stared at me like I'd grown a second head. "You're a walking disaster, you know that? Look, you need to fire him before you land yourself with a sexual harassment lawsuit, which I have zero doubts you will manage to do. Or, even if Liam is too nice a guy to press charges when his protectee gets handsy with him, it'll still be a scandal."

"He's probably not even into guys."

"Oh, he's definitely into guys," Southerland said, rolling her eyes again. "God, why are you so dumb, North? Christ."

"How do you know he's into guys?"

"I know what you're thinking. You think because you're eighteen now, it'd be all right."

I hadn't been thinking that at all. I'd just been dying to know why she was sure Liam was gay.

"It wouldn't be, though. He's your employee. He was your body-guard when you weren't eighteen—"

"He's only three years older than me."

"It doesn't matter. Hooking up with him now would be a scandal to end all scandals."

"But how do you know he's gay?" I begged.

Southerland didn't answer. She just pointed at me. "Fire him. Or I'm telling mom and dad about your crush, and they'll do it."

"What am I supposed to say?"

"Say, 'Sorry, dude, but this isn't working out. I'm letting you go, effective immediately. You'll get two weeks' severance."

"Oh, well, that's a good way to put it. But what am I supposed to tell him is the reason why?"

"You don't. In fact, giving him a reason sets you up for a wrongful termination lawsuit. Just fire him and move on."

"What should I tell Mom and Dad, though?"

"Say you didn't like the way he smelled." Southerland went back to scrolling her phone. "They'll believe that, and it's not something they can argue. I mean, what are they going to do? Tell him to shower more?"

So I'd done just what she'd said.

I could never forget the look on Liam's face when I'd sat him down and said the words "you're fired" to him. I'd thought he'd be mad or hurt or even scared because he had bills to pay, and he'd needed his job as my bodyguard to pay them.

But his eyes hadn't shown any of those things. He'd gazed at me with a softness I hadn't deserved, looking somehow proud and caring and understanding.

Or that's what I'd decided after lying in bed that night, replaying the moment over and over, trying to figure out just what his expression had meant. I'd laid around for the rest of the week, too, feeling miserable, trying to understand just *why* he'd looked at me that way. What was there be proud of? I was a coward for firing him for selfish, terrible reasons. Why didn't he get mad? Why was he still sweet to me when I was hurting him?

But Liam had left without a harsh word.

My folks hadn't argued with me when I'd told them I'd asked Liam to go. They'd just shrugged, called our security service, and Eleesha—older than Liam by five years—had taken over as my bodyguard and manager within a week.

Afterward, I tried texting Liam several times. Just small questions; easy things like: *are you okay? Did you get a new job?*

He'd never replied. Maybe he did hate me after all. Maybe he still hated me.

Eventually, I moved on with my life, blundering my way through the rest of high school and two years of college before I dropped out. Why? It wasn't just because of Robson Reynolds.

It was also because I had no direction (as my father said), and no ambition (as my mother said), and no career ideas to speak of (as my grandmother said), and no brains to put any of that together (as Southerland said). They said it was a good thing I was handsome since I'd never make any headway using my mind, but I didn't know about that.

I didn't know about a lot of things.

I wished I did.

What I knew now, though? Was that I was never going home again, I was never answering my phone again, and I was *never* leaving this quiet Christmas chalet. Because if I did, I'd have to spend the rest of my life knowing everyone I talked to had seen a picture of my dick.

I screamed into the pillow and kicked the mattress like a kid.

Turning over, I punched the soft, plush pillow again before putting my head back on it.

My dick was *mine*. It was private. It was for me to share with people I *wanted* to share it with. They'd taught me that in first grade at school, and I'd believed it ever since. And, truth be told, unless you count a few fumbling gropes with girls in those closets at parties or the rough rub Robson had given it, I'd never shared my dick with *anyone.*

I was still a virgin. Why? Because since I looked older than I was, everyone thought I was going to be a man's man in bed and dominate tiny, pretty girls or small, effeminate boys, but I didn't want that.

I wanted…

I blushed just thinking about what I wanted.

Girls or guys, I didn't want to be the one in charge or on top. I needed to be handled. I *liked* being handled.

Maybe it was because Eleesha and Liam had been so good at handling me the last many years, and I got used to it. I'd never loved it when Eleesha had taken charge of me. There was nothing erotic about her tight grip on the reins. But Liam? That was another story.

He used to handle me all the time, and I liked it. A lot. He was good at keeping me on task, keeping me focused, and always making sure I wasn't making a dumb decision that would land me in trouble with my parents or the media.

Liam did it all effortlessly.

Plus, I wanted to do everything he asked of me just because it was *him* doing the asking. Truth was, I'd spent way too many nights with my dick in my hand, wishing Liam would handle me *that* way, too. But he'd always kept his hands to himself.

No matter what Southerland said, I wasn't sure Liam even liked guys. Even if he did, what were the chances he'd like me?

But whatever the case, Liam was the only person I'd ever felt safe with, and I missed him badly. It was like I couldn't breathe right without him. If I could just have Liam here by my side, I'd be all right.

If I had more courage, I'd text him to beg for him to meet me here at the chalet. I'd ask him to come handle me. In every way. To help me feel better.

But it wasn't just courage I lacked. It was entitlement (another word Southerland had taught me). I knew a lot of guys with my background would think nothing of contacting a former employee and demanding they give up their time and attention to them again, maybe paying them for it and maybe not.

I wouldn't do that.

Grandmother Ford always said that just because we'd been born to wealth didn't mean anyone owed us anything. Grandmother Astor would cut her off by saying, "That's ridiculous! Everyone owes us everything because we create their jobs!"

Grandmother Astor's words hadn't ever reached my heart, though.

I couldn't reach out to Liam. I wouldn't. I wasn't entitled to him.

So, I'd stay here in this inn close to his hometown. I'd imagine him in his normal house, one like they show on TV, putting up a Christmas tree with his family. I'd torture myself imagining what kind of family he might have by now… A wife? A baby? A husband?

As tears slipped down my face, I rolled over to my side and stared at the long, rectangular windows cut into the dark wood of the timber walls. Mid-day light glowed across the room, sparking up the dust motes, lighting them like tiny dancing stars. They'd lift my spirits if I didn't feel hopeless.

I wiped my eyes and decided to take a nap.

My phone vibrated angrily in the drawer again.

Again. And again.

CHAPTER FOUR
Liam

I SWUNG MY truck into an empty spot outside Camp Bay Chalet, bustling now with their regular Christmas week arrivals. The rough-hewn log structure was sporting the evergreen garlands and twinkle lights Eric put up every year, and the wreath on the front door had, no doubt, been one of Jerome's creations.

When I worked here as an assistant handyman and groundskeeper during my teenage years, Camp Bay Chalet had been one of the few places where I'd felt accepted as a queer man, even before I'd been ready to accept myself. I took a moment to breathe in the cold air and take in the view of the lake and snowcapped mountains, but no more than that. If I let myself linger, I knew I'd talk myself out of doing this, and I didn't want to.

I hustled toward the front door, admiring the quaint, iced-gingerbread look of the place. The chalet sure was beautiful at Christmas.

Inside the lobby, I bypassed the small line at the front desk with Sal. The charming chatterbox saw me, and his eyes lit up. I was glad his busyness gave me an excuse to walk on by. Sal wouldn't give me the information I wanted anyway. He was too professional. Well, most of the time. I lifted my hand in greeting, continuing on through to the kitchen.

I searched for Eric.

I'd known him since he started as head of maintenance, taking the place of my old boss. Harvey had coincidentally hit retirement age right around the time Rhonda's foster brother—Eric—was let out of prison. No doubt nepotism had played a role in him being given Harvey's old position, but it'd all worked out. Harvey was able to move to Florida and be close to his daughter and grandkids, and Eric had gotten a much-needed job after a very hard time.

Back then, Eric and I had hit it off, and we'd stayed in touch ever since. If he were in town to pick up a part he needed for work, he'd hit me up to meet him for a beer, and if I could break free of Maeve's kids, I'd take him up on it. He knew enough about me to know North had been my protectee.

I found him down in the basement, an area of the house set aside for Eric's bedroom and the maintenance closets. He was in a closet now, messing around with brooms and buckets, organizing things that didn't need to be organized. He did that when he was anxious, and when we'd worked together, he'd done it a lot.

At the time, he'd been sorting through a lot of feelings related to his stint in prison, but given today's date, I could guess what he was nervous about now.

Max would arrive soon. Today or tomorrow, I'd guess.

Max was Eric's Christmas crush—or that was how I thought of him. Eric thought of Max as something else entirely: too good for him and a mistake that shouldn't have happened but one he'd love to make again. I'd never met Max, but Eric had spilled it all to me not long ago over one beer too many.

Apparently, during Max's annual visit to the inn last Christmas, he'd tugged Eric into his room, and they'd had a night to remember. Though afterward, Eric was afraid maybe Max *didn't* remember. I wasn't clear on if they'd been drinking or if Eric just thought a one-night stand with him would be unmemorable, but he worried about it a lot.

Ah, the drama we men created with our unvoiced longings and pent-up words.

I should know, having had pent-up longings for North Astor-Ford for years, and I'd never shared any words with him about it. Today that could change.

My stomach roiled like I'd had too much Christmas candy.

"Hey," I said, leaning against the door jam, peering into the depths of the closet, and taking in the well-organized shelves. I hoped I didn't look as nervous as I felt. "Looking good in here."

"Thanks." Eric wiped his palms off on his pants and reached out a hand to shake. "Long time no see."

I'd have loved to shoot the shit, but my palpitating heart and sweaty palms weren't going to let me. "Hey, I need a favor."

"What kind of favor?" Eric's little frown made me smile. He was an earnest guy, always trying to do the right thing now that he'd done the wrong thing and suffered the consequences for it. He'd always been a little suspicious of people, too.

"You remember North?"

"The too-young, former protectee you wanted to sleep with?"

"Yeah. Him."

"Sure."

"Well, he's in some trouble—"

"Again?" Eric shook his head.

"Again, yes. The thing is, he's here, in the chalet. I'd like to know which room he's staying in."

Eric crossed his arms over his chest. "He won't tell you?"

"He's not answering his phone or texts."

Eric's eyebrows flew up. "You think it's an emergency? That kind of trouble?"

I seriously doubted North was going to harm himself, but who knew anything for sure, really? The kid had to be in despair right now, and if that convinced Eric to get me his room number? Fine. "Maybe. I can't know for sure."

"Let's go." Eric motioned for me to move aside. Once I did, he strode purposely out of the closet, up the stairs, and through the kitchen, making his way to the lobby. I suspected I was going to get stuck talking with Sal after all.

I wasn't wrong.

"North Astor-Ford? Staying here?" Sal feigned surprise after the merry line of new arrivals—thankfully, folks I didn't know from my days working here—had cleared off. "Oh, honey, don't you think I *know* who he is? I recognized him the moment he sashayed in here, trying to hide away in a hoodie. Ashamed of his little scandal, I think. Not that I'd call it little. Oh, no, no. Not little at all."

North didn't "sashay," but I ignored that.

"Liam used to be his bodyguard," Eric said, gesturing toward me. "He thinks North might be in trouble and wants his room number."

Sal frowned. "Room numbers aren't public information. Let me try calling him. It'll be better to get his permission. We don't want his ridiculously rich family causing a powerful fancy problem for us, now do we?"

I shrugged, and Sal picked up the phone to ring through to North's room. He hung up when there was no answer.

"All right." He cleared his throat, looked to Eric as if to confirm I wasn't a serial killer, and said, "Well, how about Eric goes up with you? You might need a key to get in if there's no answer at the door, and Eric's maintenance key fits all the locks." He sounded anxious now, like Eric and I might discover North Astor-Ford had done something horrible to himself. The thought of that made me feel ill, too.

I reassured myself. I knew North. He was dramatic, sure, but he wouldn't take it to the extremes of despair. Hopefully.

"Just the room number is all I need. If he won't open the door for me, I'll text Eric, all right?"

"Time could be of the essence," Sal said with a pinched brow.

"Just the number, please. I don't want to overwhelm him or make him feel threatened with two guys outside his door."

Sal clucked momentarily. "I wish Rhonda were here to ask how to handle this, but she's gone at the moment. Okay, he's in 11."

"The small room?" I was surprised. North liked luxury.

"It was the only one open."

Of course. The place was always packed at Christmas. "Right. Well, if you don't hear from me, assume it's all a-okay up there."

Sal waved me off. "Go on, help that poor boy. He's too wealthy and well-endowed for anything bad to happen to him."

I snorted. Leave it to Sal to be crass despite his concern. I shook Eric's hand again. He tapped his phone in his back pocket and said, "I'm just a text away if you do find there's a problem."

"Thanks."

The ease of finding Eric and convincing Sal to give me North's room number felt like a blessing from the universe. A greater power wanted me to be here for North, even if it was just the power of the Christmas spirit.

After taking the stairs to the third floor, I rushed down the hallway with my stomach fluttering like a kid on Christmas morning. I felt juvenile and stupid, excited and worried, hopeful and anxious. Every contradictory feeling in the world jammed up inside of me until I couldn't breathe.

Stopping outside Room 11, I closed my eyes. This was it. The moment I'd longed for and dreaded for close to three years. I was going to see North again. Finally.

I knocked.

Predictably, there was no answer. I wasn't surprised since North seemed to be hiding out based on what Sal had said about him trying to conceal his face with a hoodie and the fact he wasn't answering texts or his phone.

I knocked harder.

Nothing.

"North," I called out. "I know you're in there. It's Liam. Open up."

There was a thud and a muffled curse from inside the room before the door lurched open halfway, and a red-faced North poked his head out, blue eyes wide, lush mouth open, and dark hair sticking up all around his head like he'd been pulling at it or rubbing it against a pillow while he sobbed. Probably both.

My heart creaked and cracked. The ache I'd ignored for nearly three years filled me from head to toe, and it was all I could do not to reach out and grab him in a hug, kiss his neck, and whisper in his ear that everything was going to be all right now. I'd handle this. I'd handle everything for him.

But for all I knew, he wasn't alone, *and* for all I knew, I wasn't welcome at all. He'd fired me, hadn't he? While I'd always assumed that was because he'd yearned for me the way I'd yearned for him, what if that wasn't it at all? What if he simply didn't like me or want me in his life?

Why was I suddenly doubting *everything* now I was standing in front of him? And *how* was he so ungodly handsome? Even more than when he'd been younger.

"Liam," North said, with a breathlessness that put to rest all my newly birthed fears. "It's you. You came."

"Of course, I came."

"But how did you—"

I glanced over my shoulder and saw Eric at the top of the stairs. He gave me a thumbs up, and I nodded at him. "Can I come in? Is that all right?"

"Yeah, yeah, of course. Come in." He frantically patted at his hair and smoothed a hand over his face, which was currently sporting what looked like a two-day beard. On North that was quite a lot of stubble. He still looked older than me, though I was three years his senior.

"Have a seat," he said, motioning at the plush chair in the room. After I did, he gazed around the place for a place to sit himself. There were no other options than the small desk chair, which looked like it could barely hold his tall, muscled form, or at the foot of the bed, so he took the latter, shifting around awkwardly. He pushed his hair out of his face and then messed it up again.

"Um..." North began, swallowing hard and gazing at me with wide eyes full of wild, tumbling emotions. I could relate to them all. "I guess you saw."

"Are you alright?"

North's eyes filled with tears, and he swallowed convulsively. He rose and walked to the other window, and gazed out.

I knew from the position of the room and my prior years at the chalet he was looking at the winding road and the scrub of a wintery mountainside. The mountain always appeared magical, even if some of the snowfall was dripping away in this unseasonable warmth. The trees outside creaked as I waited in silence, and out in the hallway, a couple of enthusiastic voices passed by.

Eventually, North spoke. "I'm not okay, no. I'm embarrassed and humiliated." He wiped at his face, keeping his back to me. "Did you see it?"

I ignored the question and asked my own. "It was an accident?"

"Of course it was!" he spat out, shoulders tensing. "Did you think it wasn't? That I'd post my dick on purpose?"

"No, I didn't. I'd never think that."

"Then why'd you ask?" His voice shook.

"Because I don't know what happened exactly. For all I knew, someone else posted it to your account, or you were hacked. But I do know *you*, North, and I was certain you didn't put up a picture like that on purpose. I also knew you'd be hurting, so I reached out as soon as I could."

"You did?"

"Yeah, and when I got no answer, I came to find you."

North glanced at me out of the corner of his eye. The light from the window illuminated his lashes, stroked over his lush lips, and made his entire face glow like an angel. "How did you know I was here?"

I decided to be honest. "You never removed me from the Find My iPhone app, and I never suggested I be removed…"

"Ah."

My stomach hurt witnessing his pain. I wanted to make it go away. "When I saw the news today, and I texted, and when you didn't answer, and it didn't show as read, my worry got the best of me."

"So you looked to see where I was."

"Yeah, just to reassure myself, make sure you were with family or friends. That kind of thing. Imagine my surprise when I saw you were *here*." I kept the question about why, exactly, he'd come here of all places to myself for now. "When I saw you were here at the chalet, I didn't think. I just got into my car and came to you. I hope you don't feel like I've violated your privacy."

North's shoulders loosened. "No. I've always known you could still see where I was. On the app, I mean." Blushing, he cleared his throat. "I liked imagining you cared where I was and what I might be doing."

"I did. I do."

North ducked his head, his voice going rough. "Even though I fired you and ruined your life?"

I chuckled. "You didn't ruin my life. Only I could have done that, and maybe, if you hadn't fired me, I would have."

He turned halfway again. His gorgeous profile was outlined by the sun through the window. He was like art, and I wanted to breathe him in. "How would you have ruined your life?"

I calculated in my head all the evidence of the three years I'd spent with him and the doubts that'd consumed my mind as I'd waited to knock earlier and weighed them together until the sum was clear. What did I have to lose now? If it upset him, if he wanted me to go, I'd go.

I took the risk. "Maybe, if you hadn't fired me, I'd have acted on my feelings for you at some point, which *would* have ruined my life. You had just turned teen, and I was your bodyguard and manager, in a position of authority over you—"

"You were *my* employee," North disagreed. "Southerland said it would have been my fault if something happened. She said I'd have been sexually harassing *you*."

I smiled. "She would say that."

North turned to me fully, the backlighting from the window blocking out his features. I couldn't easily read his face, but I didn't need to. I knew him so well; even now, the nuances of his voice told me everything. "She was wrong?"

"No, and yes. But it doesn't matter. You were right to let me go, and I never held it against you. But I'm here now because I do care for you, and I can't let you suffer alone when I can offer my support." I lifted my hands in a self-effacing shrug.

North stepped closer, hesitated, and sat again on the foot of the bed across from my chair; his breath came in shallow gasps, and his eyes had dilated despite their recent exposure to strong sunlight. So many emotions rolled over his face I couldn't begin to pick them all out. "Okay," he said simply after we'd both stared at each other for a long time. He rubbed his arms and tore his gaze from mine. "You're here."

"Yes."

"Now what?"

I glanced toward the dresser, where rapid-fire rattling had been sounding off and on since I entered the room. It vibrated again like a rattlesnake was in the drawer trying to get out. I knew what it was and why it was in there because, as I said, I knew North. "Now we deal with your phone."

He groaned and rubbed both hands over his face, scrubbing over his beard growth and collapsing back on the mattress dramatically. "Not yet."

"Everything else will be easier once that's handled."

"*Not yet*," he repeated.

I sat in silence for a moment, letting him think and breathe, letting him get used to me being there in the room with him. I took a moment to get used to it myself. His scent was familiar and wonderful to me. I took it in—his subtle vanilla and wood odor I was pretty sure came from his designer shampoo, and his own anxious sweat stink I was familiar with as well from years of him tripping into trouble.

"If you don't want to handle it now, why haven't you silenced your phone?"

North averted his eyes. "I don't remember how."

"You could have looked it up online. They have video tutorials for everything on YouTube."

"I'm *not* looking online!"

"Right, of course not." I rose. "I'll deal with it."

North sat up and grabbed my hand, pulling me toward him. "Don't you want to know why I came here? To this place?"

"I assume you're hiding out," I said, not wanting to express my true hopes for fear I'd embarrass myself by being wrong or that he'd deny it.

"Yeah, I am, but…" He stared at me and ran his gaze from my head to my feet and back again. "You're really here. You actually came."

"Didn't you think I would?"

"No. Well, I'd hoped. That was *why* I came here. To Camp Bay

Chalet. Because I really wanted to see you. I wanted you to tell me it was going to be okay, like how you used to do, but…" A bitter smile touched his lips as he dropped my wrist. "But I was a coward then, and I'm a coward now, so I just checked in here at your old workplace instead of going to your mom's house to find you."

"There were closer hotels in Sandpoint proper." I sat again, leaning forward, elbows on my knees.

"Yeah, but I remembered how you said this was a great place. Accepting. I'd hoped it would be a safe place for me, too." Pink appeared again on his cheeks above his beard. "I'd hoped it'd be somewhere I could stay until all this mess disappears."

"It won't disappear until we deal with your phone." It rattled again like it sensed I was talking about it.

"Not now."

I said nothing more, crossing my legs and leaning back in the chair. I affected a patient nonchalance I didn't feel. I wanted to move over to the bed, push him back to the mattress, climb over him, straddle his hips, and kiss him until he was breathless and clinging to me. Preferably naked.

But now wasn't the time, and it was way too soon in the scheme of everything to even be thinking such thoughts. I didn't know where his head was at or what we needed to do to fix all this. Or at least attempt to.

First things first.

"Didn't you hear me?" North asked, tilting his head, gaze boring in me. "I *wanted* you. I came here for *you*. I had your address at your mom's house from when I googled it after you left, and I was going to just show up, but I couldn't."

"Why not? And don't say it's because you're a coward. Because you're not."

"I was afraid you hated me. That, and Southerland said I've got to be careful not to be entitled, which means I can't assume I'm allowed access to you or your help after what I did to you."

"You didn't do anything to me."

"I fired you! And made you move back in with your mother! Even though you say I didn't, I know I messed up your life by being—"

"By being what? Too attractive?" I smiled. "North, I meant it when I said the feeling went both ways. It was a powder keg that was going to explode. I should have manned up and left months before you fired me. I was never angry with you. Not for a minute."

"I missed you." North's voice was ragged and miserable. "I really missed you a lot."

"I missed you, too."

The space between us felt electric, like either one or both of us would ignite if we moved into it. I held my breath and let it settle before I said, "There's plenty more to discuss on that topic, but I hate to tell you, baby—we're gonna have to work through this crisis first." I pointed toward the rattling drawer. "Go get your phone."

CHAPTER FIVE
North

*B*ABY. HE'D SAID it so easily. The word made me feel like crying. I'd never felt like I was anyone's baby, not even my mom's. Was I allowed to be his? Did he really want me to be? What did it even mean that he'd called me something that sweet?

I had a lot of questions, maybe because I was an idiot. Other guys would probably just *know* what he meant by it. Other guys would—

Wait. Other guys?

Or girls?

Or people?

I chewed my bottom lip for a moment, but the phone was vibrating so loudly I couldn't think. I hauled myself off the bed with a mumbled curse and ripped open the drawer, retrieving my enraged iPhone. It buzzed in my palm like a handful of bees.

"Now what?" I asked, staring at it with fear and disgust.

Liam was steady and sure. Everything I'd always loved—*liked*—about him. "Give it to me."

I did.

"Is the password still the same?"

It was.

Liam moved to the bed and gestured for me to sit beside him. Obeying, I wondered if he could feel me trembling—with fear, excitement, and joy he was here? All of the above? Yes.

Liam thumbed in the password, and I gulped as the screen filled with notifications. "Who do you want to call first?" he asked.

I didn't hesitate. There was only one person I could even think of talking with right now, even though she'd probably scold me too. "Southerland."

"All right." Liam took hold of my hand and squeezed it. My fingers were sweaty, and his were dry, rock solid. I never wanted to let him go. "Let's do this."

"No." I surprised myself by saying it, but I needed a few answers first. I wasn't patient like him.

"Baby, we need to call—"

"Do you have a girlfriend?" I blurted, my stomach turning over as I snatched the phone from him. I gripped it tightly, and the PopSocket dug into my palm.

What if his "baby" was meant as fatherly? Patern—what was the word? Paternal? Yeah, paternal. Liam said he'd had feelings for me in the *past*, not that he had them for me *now*.

I mean, he'd implied it, but as my family had told me a million times over the years, I wasn't always the brightest bulb on the Christmas tree, and I couldn't always count on my own interpretation of things.

"No," Liam said, a smile moving across his lips. They weren't especially full, not like mine, but there was something satisfying and comforting in their firm shape. Thin, but not too thin. Straight but easily curved up with a smile at the sides. I'd always wanted to have his kiss.

"No?" I asked to make sure I'd heard right.

"I'm gay, North."

Holy shit. He was gay. I rubbed the back of my neck, a cold, excited chill sweeping me. "Southerland thought so."

"She would."

"And do you, um…" My heart was pounding, my breath sucking in way too fast. I gasped the rest of the words out. "Do you have a boyfriend?"

Liam's brows went up. "Do you?"

"No!"

"A girlfriend?" His cinnamon-brown gaze pierced me. "Is she who you meant to send the picture to?"

"No!"

"Then who?"

"A hookup, but not a real hookup. An online thing. A guy," I babbled. "But you didn't say if you have a boyfriend or not. Answer me."

"No, I don't have a boyfriend."

"Have you ever?"

"I've had a few."

Irrational annoyance zipped through me. "How many?"

Liam laughed. "We need to focus. There's time for all this later."

"How many boyfriends?" I insisted.

"Five."

"Five!" I threw my hands up. "How? When?"

"Christ. Let's deal with your phone and—"

"*When* did you have five boyfriends?"

Liam's sigh was exasperated. "Two during high school. One during protection training. And, yes, I dated a couple of guys while I was guarding you."

"How?" I'd kept him very busy. When had he found the time? Besides, he'd lived with me! In my boarding school dorm and in my house! How could I not have known this?

"I had days off."

"You fucked other guys on your days off?" I gritted the question out, my blood pounding and my head feeling like it was about to pop off. Ugly jealousy. I was familiar with it, but not like this. Not like I could puke or burst into tears or both.

"North…"

"Did you?"

"Yes."

"But earlier, you said you had feelings for me back then!"

Liam sighed. He smelled like spearmint gum, and I wanted to punch him and kiss him, or maybe I wanted to shove him down and rub all over him until I smelled like that too.

"I did have feelings for you," Liam said. "But I knew they weren't appropriate. I tried to drown them out by dating other men. It didn't work."

"But you slept with them anyway."

"I did." Liam tilted his head. "I'm sure you've slept with your fair share of people. Were you in love with every last one of them?"

"I've never slept with *anyone*," I said fiercely as if I'd been guarding my virginity or something, which wasn't true at all. I'd have fucked any number of people given the right circumstances and signed NDAs, but I didn't want Liam to know that. I wanted him to feel bad for touching those other guys.

Liam's brows rose again, but this time in surprise. "But you're—"

"I've never fucked anyone," I repeated. "At all."

"Oh."

I considered letting him twist for a moment, but his confused and lost expression was too much for me. I blurted, "Because the lawyers practically scared me out of *masturbating* in case it somehow got leaked to the tabloids that I'd touched my own dick. I couldn't risk real sex. Until I *did* risk it. I mean, kind of. It wasn't real—like no one touched me. It was just on this app. But I was *so* careful about it. I was."

"I believe you."

"I used an alias and a fake picture, and I never told anyone who I really was or met them in person. I was *careful*-careful."

"Because of the thing at Halloween?"

"You know about that?"

"Hard to miss it. I'm glad he wasn't your boyfriend. I was worried for you—concerned about the kind of people you were hanging out with."

"He wasn't my boyfriend. We weren't even friends."

"I'm sorry. That had to be a rough time for you, too."

"Why didn't you come check on me?"

"Because I thought maybe you'd hire Eleesha back afterward or at least hire *someone*."

"She told you I fired her?"

"Of course. We're friends. Graduated from the same protection program, and she sometimes texted me to ask how I'd handle certain issues with you. That kind of thing."

"You were still watching out for me?"

"Of course, but there was only so much I could do from afar, and I didn't want to interfere in your life if I wasn't wanted."

"I wanted you. Even after I fired you."

"You wanted me while you were kissing girls in closets at your senior year parties?"

"You heard about that, too?"

"Eleesha was a snitch." Liam chuckled.

"What else did she tell you?"

"That you threw away the NDAs I told her to get for you. She told me you were propositioned right and left by men your father's age, some of your father's colleagues even in the movie business, and worse."

I shivered. "Ugh. Those old assholes. As if I'd let them touch me."

"But there were people you wanted to touch, weren't there? Men and women, girls and guys?"

I swallowed. "Yeah."

"Then you understand."

"Maybe." I clenched my jaw. "I don't like it, though."

Liam laughed. "Well, a few years ago, I imagined you out sowing wild oats, sleeping with guys and girls and professors and whoever else, and if it makes you feel better, it used to bother me a lot."

My heart thumped to imagine Liam thinking of me…doing sexy things. Did he still want to do that? Not just think about it, but… "Eleesha should have told you about me, about how I never slept with anyone. She knew."

"Eleesha is a gossip, but she has limits."

I groaned, pushing my hands through my hair. "I *wish* I'd sown oats!"

"I wish you had, too. Even if I don't love the thought of you with other men or women, it doesn't mean it wouldn't have been healthy for you. Every young man needs some wild years."

I shrugged. "I don't know. Maybe it's good I didn't do any sowing. I'm bad with needles." I met his gaze, which shone with amusement for some reason. "And, in general, I think getting wild is overrated."

Liam smiled again, his winning, handsome grin which made my heart jolt. "Oh yeah? Why's that?"

"I've had plenty of experience with the consequences of being wild, even when I haven't actually *been* wild. It sucks. I don't want any of it."

It wasn't entirely true; a week ago, I'd have said something very different to nearly anyone else. But looking at Liam, with his freckled face, his gorgeous brown eyes, and his red hair which he always kept neat and would look really great messed up from my hands, I meant it when I went on to say, "I just care about you."

Liam took a quick breath. "You're a sweet kid."

"I'm not a kid anymore."

Before I could prove to him just how grown-up I was—or

wanted to be, at least—the phone jolted to life in my hand, and while trying to not drop it, I apparently swiped and answered the call.

"Holy shit, you enormous idiot, where the fuck have you been?" My sister's face filled the phone's screen, brown eyes wide, brows raised, and her autumn-leaves-colored hair tugged back in a ponytail. "I mean, I know *where* you are. They've tracked you. But why?"

"This is the inn Liam worked at when he was younger."

Southerland's eyebrows did a dance. "You're with Liam?"

I glanced toward him, and my stomach flipped wildly. *He's here. He's really here with me.* "Yes."

"Wow, okay, he's there right now with you?"

"Yes." At Liam's nod, I briefly angled the screen so Southerland could see him sitting beside me. Liam gave her a little salute.

Southerland blew out a long breath, shoved the loose ends of hair back from her face, and tightened her ponytail before sitting upright and saying, "Okay, well, good. You're both legal, and you're not his boss now. I guess whatever happens, happens, and he's *got* to be better for you than Robson fucking Reynolds."

"I never dated him!" And just like that, an avalanche of humiliation crashed into me again. Liam hesitantly touched my knee as tears came to my eyes. The warm pressure of his hand felt like it was keeping me from cracking into a million pieces.

Southerland cracked a smile. "I know you didn't. Christ. Calm down. Can't you take a little teasing?"

"No. Not really. Not today anyway." I dashed the stupid tears away.

Southerland's expression softened. "All right, yeah, I should go easy on you. Though, really, on the other hand, *why should I, North?*" Her voice rose. "This is easily one of the most traumatizing things to ever happen to me, you realize. I've had to see your…your…junk, *ugh*, over and over and over. It's on every social media feed, and my asshole friends keep texting it to me. I might go gay over this myself, you realize. I mean, now when I think of hard dicks, yours is what's going to come to mind, and *ugh*, gag, gross. Trauma. PTSD. I need therapy."

"We all need therapy," I said because it was true. Beside me, Liam snorted softly, and I sensed his agreement.

"Yes, well, hell." Southerland sighed and pushed her loose hair back again. "Mom and Dad have a plan. I think it's a good one, but knowing you, and I do, you're gonna refuse it."

"What plan?"

"They want you to claim you were hacked and say it's not your dick."

"Smart," Liam said. "That's what I'd suggest, too."

"But it *is* my dick!" I exclaimed.

"Lying isn't always bad, North." Southerland blew out another exasperated breath.

"Of course, not everyone will believe it," Liam said. "I mean, don't get me wrong, it's a good plan, but at most, it'll divide the camps. You'll have those who believe it actually is North's dick, and this is all a coverup—which is the truth—and there'll be those who think he *was* hacked, and it's not his dick—"

"It is my dick!"

"I know, baby," Liam said, and I shivered again at the pet name.

I kind of loved it. It meant something, right? People didn't just go around calling each other "baby" for no reason. I hoped he called me baby forever and ever and ever, and held me down and did everything I'd always imagined, and—

Wait, no, I needed to focus. He was saying something else now.

"It doesn't matter if it's your dick. What matters is if we can cast doubt on it being your dick."

"The third camp will be those who think he *was* hacked, but it *is* his dick," Southerland finished.

"Yes," Liam agreed.

"So two-thirds of the people will still think it's my dick?" Look at me doing math. And Mrs. Drumm, my high school math instructor, always said I was hopeless at it.

"But one-third will be sure it's not," Southerland said. "Which is better than one hundred percent of the whole world thinking it's definitely your dick."

"The whole world…" I murmured. "The whole entire world has seen my dick."

"I'm sure there's someone in Bangladesh who hasn't seen it yet but give them a few hours."

I croaked, "Mom saw it?"

"Of course."

I wiped my hand over my face. "And Grandma?"

"Ford or Astor?"

"Either?"

"Both."

I cringed. "I can't ever look them in the face again."

"No, especially not Grandma Astor, who's probably going to cut you out of her will—"

"Southerland," Liam scolded.

"She might," she said with a smirk. "But it's unlikely since, somehow, despite it all, he's still her favorite. Must be nice to be so pretty; even the evil grandma loves you best."

"You're pretty," I said, because she was and because Grandma Astor was a bitch. She might love me more than she loved Southerland, but she also hated me plenty, and we all knew it. I just didn't want to think about either of my grandmothers seeing that picture. It showed my entire hard dick! They shouldn't ever have seen it!

"Whatever. Anyway, Grandma Ford is 'troubled.'"

"What's that mean?"

"She's worried about you. You should call her next."

I was definitely *not* calling my grandmother ever again. "But what about Mom and Dad?"

"They're fine." Southerland rolled her eyes. "They've been following you on the surveillance apps, and they figured you were with Liam."

"You already knew he was here?"

"We assumed. It's not like your crush on him has ever been a big secret."

"Mom and Dad thought I fired him because of the way he smells!"

Liam squawked. "The way I *smell?*"

"You smell fine," I reassured him. "Great even. Like spearmint and—"

"Ugh, not now," Southerland muttered. "Mom and Dad are not the idiots they appear to be, and they knew all along you wanted Liam to bang you like a gong."

"Why'd you tell me to lie to them then?"

"Because it amused me, and I knew they'd never believe it anyway."

I said nothing. What was there to say? I was the dummy who'd fallen for it and thought for all these years, my folks believed Liam smelled like coconut. I hated the smell of coconut.

"Mom and Dad think it's good you're there with him. They know he'll keep you from getting into any more trouble."

"How would I get into *more* trouble? It's not like I'm going to send another picture out from a better angle!"

Southerland shivered. "Ugh. You are gross. How did you even make this big of a mistake?"

I explained the whole story to her, and she started to laugh about halfway through.

"HungryTop34, are you *kidding me?* Are you saying these words right now? To your kid sister? In front of your boyfriend?"

My face burned. "Liam's not my boyfriend."

"Isn't he, though?"

Liam was suspiciously quiet, and I didn't say anything more, either.

"Whatever. So you were trying to message this pic to a guy you were having an online hookup with, and boom! You sent it all over the world! Social media cross-posting shit-show!"

"Yes."

"Oh, North." She rubbed her face. "I think Grandma Ford would say—"

"Don't."

"Bless your heart."

I rolled my eyes. Grandma Ford's Southernism for "honey, you're dumb as rocks" had been directed at me more than once in my life. "How bad is it? Really?"

"Oh, it's bad. The attorneys are writing screeds. They've got computer gurus trying to erase the unerasable. They have drafts of apologies and drafts of denials. Mom and Dad have been drinking and fighting all day. Good times."

"I'm sorry."

"You should be. You caused this mess, and I'm the one here dealing with the fallout while you are hiding away with your hot new boyfriend."

"He's not—" I cut myself off because I wanted him to be. "Stop. We haven't even really talked about stuff. He says I have to handle all this first."

"Good, Liam," she called out. "You've always done what's right. Except for when you made me be the one to talk my brother into firing you instead of doing the right thing and quitting yourself. Me, a sixteen-year-old kid at the time, mind you."

"Sorry, Southerland," Liam said, his soft but firm voice not sounding sorry at all. "I'm not perfect."

"I guess you're close enough, or at least my folks think so, which is good since it'll be easier to be with North with their approval. Not that he wouldn't buck the family for you. I'm sure he would, but—" She broke off at a knock on her bedroom door. "Hold on. It's Mom."

She disappeared from the screen, and I was simultaneously hyperaware of Liam's breathing beside me and what I could make out of Southerland's side of the call. I heard her open the door. I heard Mom's voice, muffled but easy enough to understand, "Are you talking with him?"

"Yes."

"Have him call me. Now."

"I will. He's just getting the lay of the land. You know how it is. Wants to know just how bad things are before facing you."

"Just tell him to call your dad or me. Immediately."

"Have you been drinking, Mom? You look like you've been hitting the booze." Southerland laughed and shut the door. She appeared back on the screen, lying across her bed. "She has been. Martinis, I think. Get ready! She's feeling *feelings*, North. Not sure what kind, but she didn't look angry, at least."

"What about Dad?"

"Oh, he's been boozing since he got up. Bloody Marys followed by manhattans followed by more manhattans."

"Great."

"It's better when they're drunk, though," she said, and it wasn't a lie. "They're softer."

"I guess."

"Though, this time? They're pretty mad too. Who knows what you're actually going to get out of them? You better go ahead and call."

My heart thumped. "All right."

"The worst that happens is they yell at you and make you record an apology for their lawyers to upload. I mean, even if they go with the hacking thing, you're going to have to apologize for—" she waved her hand around—"being hacked, I guess. That's how it works, right?"

"I don't think I can lie on camera," I muttered. "Everyone will know."

"True. So don't lie."

"But if they make me—"

"Just don't tell the truth. There's a difference."

"No, there isn't."

"Oh, North. Christ. Just follow the script. They'll have one prepared." Another knock came on her door. "He's going to call you! Just a second!" She peered into the camera at me and muttered, "I love you, dummy. Call them."

The screen went dark.

Liam shifted slightly nearer to me, his hand still warm and perfect on my knee. I wanted to turn into his arms, kiss him, lose myself in lust and forget all about how my parents were going to call me any second if I didn't call them first.

Liam moved first. He stood, ran his hands over my hair, and said, "Let's do it. Let's get this part done."

His sexy smile said if I got through this call with my folks, he was going to strip me naked. At least, that was my interpretation?

God, I hoped I was right for once in my life.

When my dad and mom's faces appeared, I didn't know if I had the strength to follow through without hanging up. And when they both started yelling at once, I closed my eyes and reached out for Liam's hand.

He gave it willingly, and I squeezed, letting my parents' voices tumble over me.

CHAPTER SIX

Liam

NORTH'S PARENTS HADN'T changed a bit. They were both entirely focused on themselves and how North's penis's journey around the world might affect their careers, their reputations, their feelings, their social standing, how many people were likely to attend tomorrow's Christmas charity ball, and more.

North was, as usual, adorable in how he tried to handle them, but there was no way he was going to get a word in edgewise. Not with them both screaming at him like that. I sat beside him, visible on the screen but apparently unimportant to Ms. Astor and Mr. Ford while they ranted.

"I'm sorry!" North burst out for the fifth time. "I didn't mean to!"

"Didn't mean to? What does that even mean?" Mrs. Astor screeched, but, typical of her when she felt her social standing being shaken at the roots by some mishap of her son's, she didn't even let him answer. "You certainly had to 'mean it' to take that picture." She covered her face dramatically and shook her head as her husband took over the panic-laced beratement.

"Do you know what this is going to cost us in attorneys' fees and technological guru fees and whatever else is necessary to get your enormous prick off the damn internet?"

Enormous was right. What would it feel like in—

I stopped that thought. I couldn't get lost in the gooey, wonderous feeling of being with North now. I needed to muscle him through this bad spot so we could get down to the business of letting me experience the enormity of his cock in my mouth, my ass, and anywhere else on my body he wanted to put it.

My face flushed as the heat of my imaginings lit me up inside. I tried to push it aside, but my mind kept drifting away from the Astor-Fords' endless woe-is-me-ing, and back to all the ways I could take North apart on this bed and all the things I could be the first to teach him.

I *would* be the first to teach him. From the moment he'd opened the door, I think we both knew. There was nothing standing between us now. Aside from this torturous video call.

I had enough right about the time Deacon called North an idiot. Which, bless his beautiful face and angelic heart, he absolutely was—but he was my idiot, and I wouldn't stand by and let his dad hurt him any longer. Deacon Ford didn't pay my salary anymore. I had nothing to lose by speaking up.

"That's enough!" I burst out, tilting the iPhone screen toward me, leaving North on the peripheral. "Mr. Ford, Mrs. Astor, it's time to put aside all these feelings and do something about the situation. What do the attorneys suggest? An apology, I'm assuming?"

"Oh—" Deacon looked flustered, but he didn't seem offended. Which was good, but I saw Susan blink rapidly, likely insulted by my input. "Yes, as a matter of fact, they do."

"All right, and our understanding is North is going to assert the falsehood that his phone was hacked, and those were not his genitals in the picture."

Susan sucked in a breath as if she were being subjected to the picture of her son's dick all over again.

"That's right," Deacon confirmed.

"Great. North has agreed to take this path of least resistance—"

"It *is* my dick, though," North whispered beside me, his thick brows lowering in frustration.

"It's still going to be your dick even if we say it isn't," I assured him. I really wanted him to make this choice on his own.

"Okay," North said, but he sounded small. I squeezed his thigh reassuringly.

"Send the various speeches the attorneys have prepared, and I'll help him choose the right one or the right combination of one."

"You'll record it at once," his father said, pointing a finger at the screen.

"Cry some if you can," Susan added. "Play up how humiliated you are. The audience will have sympathy for you."

"I *am* humiliated," North murmured. "It's not an act."

"For heaven's sake, ignore your mother," Deacon burst out. "Do not cry; do you hear me? No one wants to see a man cry. It's repulsive."

"It's vulnerable!" Susan exclaimed. "People will eat it up."

Next to me, North was shaking, and when I turned to look at his profile, I saw him manfully trying to suck his tears back through his eyeballs. It broke my heart to know he was hurt, and they, his parents, had no empathy for his pain.

"Let's get on with it," I encouraged, wanting to get the phone call over so I could take North in my arms and tell him he could cry anytime, and I wouldn't find it repulsive. I'd hold him through his tears and kiss them away if he let me.

That was when Susan glanced toward Deacon, who nodded at her, and she sighed. "Liam, you must know how much we've always trusted you with our son. We'd like you to consider being at his side in the future. You were always good with him."

They were talking about him like he was a troublesome toddler.

"And we know you care for him—"

I blinked, a panicked denial on my lips, but I swallowed it back. I didn't have anything to be ashamed of—North was an adult now, and I was only three years older than him. I'd never crossed a boundary when I was his bodyguard. It was fine.

Besides, both Deacon and Susan were looking at me with approval in their eyes. I supposed the fact that I was with North right now was proof I cared for him on a personal level.

"We know you've always had his best interests at heart, and we were disappointed when he chose to let you go when he was younger."

"Though it was the right thing to do," Deacon said sternly. "He was far too crazy about you. Can you imagine the rumors? The damage to our reputations had we let you both act on your feelings?" He clutched his chest. "This dick pic is nothing compared to the scandal that would have brought to the family."

"Our attorneys told us if North hadn't let you go, we'd have needed to fire you ourselves. What if we'd allowed it, and word had gotten out?"

"Can you imagine the impact on your reputation?" I asked with an edge I didn't expect them to catch, and they didn't.

"Exactly," she said, shaking her brunette bob and pressing the side of her cocktail glass against her cheek, apparently letting the coolness soothe her. "Embarrassing." Her eyes shot open. "Just like this picture is embarrassing and—"

"I assure you; I was never going to act inappropriately with your son while I was under your employ. Now let's focus on getting this handled," I said again, keeping my tone even, though I wanted to reach through the screen and shake her.

How these people could care more about their feelings than their son's right now, I didn't know. He was here next to me, looking miserable and sick, but they didn't even ask how he was doing.

"Right," Deacon said to Susan like he'd been trying to convince her of this for hours now, and she was simply being difficult.

"As I said, email the scripts. I'll see that the attorneys have a copy of his apology soon. If they approve, they can upload it. I assume they still have his passwords from the last time they needed to get into his accounts?"

"They do."

"Good. That's all we need." I turned to North and whispered, "Is that everything you need from them?"

North nodded, looking toward the screen again with a wounded expression on his face. "I'm sorry."

"Never again!" Susan said, standing up and striding away.

"Like your mother said." Deacon's eyebrows were high and angular, almost like he was pointing them at North.

He disconnected the call.

"They're so mad," North said, his voice shaking. "They wouldn't even let me explain."

"I know. I'm sorry."

"I wanted a chance to explain."

"You deserved that." I pulled him into my arms and stroked his dark hair, lightly humming as I rubbed my freshly shaven cheek against his stubble.

"Liam?"

"Mmm?"

"Will you...can you...?"

"Can I what, baby?"

"Kiss me?"

My heart thudded as I pulled away enough to gaze into his pleading eyes. I didn't leave him hanging. I pressed my lips to his and, just like that, the world went topsy-turvy. My pulse rushed in my ears, and my body trembled as I was overcome with the joy and wonder of finally having his mouth on mine.

With a noise of want, North opened his lips and let my tongue in. If North had been kissing those girls in the closets as Eleesha claimed, he hadn't learned much during those experiences. His mouth was inexpert, teeth clashing against mine, and his canine sliding against my lip painfully.

My dick didn't care. It strained against my jeans as my heart pounded at my ribcage. Stars burst behind my closed eyelids from finally, *finally* touching him, putting my mouth on his glorious mouth, and hearing his low, excited noises. Still, another strangling press of his tongue into my mouth was enough for me to pull away, panting.

"Wait," I whispered. "Let me just…" I positioned his head, rubbing my nose against his before planting a soft kiss against his slick lips. "Let me show you."

North gripped my back with both hands, his eyes closed, squeezed tight with a desperate desire for more, or maybe in embarrassment at needing to be coached, but he said nothing as I taught him how to be soft with his mouth.

Kissing each lip, sucking in the bottom one before working his mouth open to slip my tongue inside, dancing it gently against the sensitive parts of his mouth, I demonstrated how good a kiss could be.

North shuddered against me, clenching me harder. I fought the urge to shove his shirt up to play with his nipples, trying to focus on not escalating this kiss beyond what I could endure because we still had much more to deal with before we could take this to its natural conclusion. A conclusion I definitely had no doubts about.

We both wanted each other.

We were going to get off together.

Pulling back, I smiled as North leaned in, trying to catch my mouth again. "Shh." I pressed a finger to his now swollen and slick lips. "More of that later. We need to deal with this apology."

"Nooo," he moaned. "I'm so horny."

I chuckled, pressing kisses to his neck, his Adam's apple, and his hot cheeks. His stubble scraped against my lips, and I couldn't help but imagine how it might feel brushing against other, more sensitive parts. But not now—

"You're going to come for me, baby," I whispered. "Soon. But not until we've handled this video."

"Come for you?" North's eyes opened wide, and he stared at me in a daze of lust. "I can come for you?"

I slipped my hands into his hair and pondered whether or not he was going to be able to focus without getting off first. It would be easy enough to pleasure him. I could press him back on the bed, climb on top of him, and gyrate—he'd be jizzing his jeans in a heartbeat. The idea made *my* pulse throb, and suddenly I wanted nothing more than to do it.

"Come on," I murmured, drawn to kissing his lips again, licking the corners, touching my tongue to his tongue, and pulling away, blinking back to sanity again. "Let's do this."

"No," North whispered, shaking his head. "I waited so long to have you. I'm not going to wait anymore."

"Have me?" The words pricked my curiosity. "What are you going to do to me?"

North shook his head again. "That's not the question," he said cheekily. "It's what you're going to do to me."

"I'm going to do it to you?" The idea of topping him, of getting my hands on him, and my dick in his incredibly well-sculpted ass was a rush. I didn't know if I could wait. I didn't know if I *should*.

Well, I knew I should—we had to film the apology, but…

"Yes," North hissed. "Do it to me. Please. I want you to be my first."

I smiled, something about the phrasing tickling me. "Oh? Your first? Who do you have in mind for your second?"

North's breath came in shakily. "You again."

"That's better," I murmured, going in for another kiss, and this time I did press him back against the bed. He wrapped his arms around my back, and I started a rough roll of my hips, pressing my aching cock against his through our jeans. "Go on and come for me now, baby. You'll feel much better once you do."

North whined and clutched at me, pulling at my shirt, breathing loud and rough against my ear. "That's good," I murmured. "You're almost there. I've got you."

"Liam," he grunted, his fingers digging into my sides. "I'm going to, oh...oh!" Strangled sounds of pleasure came from him as he buried his face against my shoulder and shuddered. I kissed his hair, his cheeks, and his lips again, whispering encouragement. "Give me your cum. You're so hot. C'mon, yes."

He growled as a final spasm ripped through him. Surging up, he kissed me himself. The kiss wasn't much better, but he was desperate, and I went with it until both of our lips were red and aching.

"Did you come?" he asked me as I rolled off him and examined the wet spot on his jeans.

"No," I whispered. "I'm saving my cum for you to swallow."

He stared at me a moment, licked his lips, and whispered, "Swallow?"

I touched his eyebrows, smoothing them with my thumb. "I'm seven months out from the last time I had sex with anyone. I'm on PrEP. You're a virgin. Do we need condoms? I can get some if you want. It's not a problem."

"No," he moaned. "I want to. Please let me suck you."

I grinned. "Oh, North. I'm so glad you're here. *Fuck.*"

We kissed some more, and I had a hard time keeping my promise not to come, especially when I opened his pants, pulled his cock free, and gave him a handjob.

North was immediately lost in it. He stared at me or tried to with his eyes falling shut as his face twisted up with pleasure and lust. His dick was still sloppy from his first orgasm, slicked with his cum. The wet noise of my hand working him and the scent of his sweat rose up around us. I greedily watched his face as he cried out and exploded a second time. "That's my baby," I encouraged. "You're so good at that."

North's gulped and gasped, his hips shuddering with each jerk of his cock. Cum flew up over his shirt and splattered his face. I leaned forward to lick it off, and when I pulled back, he was staring at me like I was a superhero or a god.

Did I mention I had a bit of a hero complex?

CHAPTER SEVEN
North

UNFORTUNATELY, THE ORGASMS didn't last forever. (Orgasms with *Liam*!) Underneath his adorable freckles, Liam was apparently a sex god *and* a cruel demon who was a stickler for keeping me on track.

After the mind-numbing orgasms nearly wiped my memory of how much crap I was in right now—and *kissing*! So much kissing!—he made me clean up, put on sweats and a T-shirt from my bag, and sit down to record the apology.

I had a hard time concentrating on learning the words my parents' attorneys wanted me to say. My greatest fantasy had just come true. I'd shot for Liam. Twice! And he'd held me through the pleasure, looking like he'd enjoyed my climaxes as much as I had.

As Liam tweaked the speech the attorneys had sent and read it aloud to me for a third time, I barely heard him. All I could do was shake and shiver, giggling when I wasn't gasping with disbelief.

"Baby, you need to concentrate," Liam said, coming to sit by my side again.

"I can't," I said with a bubbly laugh. "I can't believe this is real."

Liam smiled, cradling the back of my head and bringing our foreheads together. "It's real. And it can be even more real when this apology is done and dusted."

"More real?"

"Yes."

"Are you sure this isn't a dream? Because last night was the worst of my whole life, but now I'm here with you, and you kissed me, and you made me come." I shivered, and he did too. "Tell me I'm awake."

"You're awake."

"Tell me you want me, for real."

"I want you, North. But I also want you to record this apology."

"Let's just have more sex."

Liam laughed. "Tempting, believe me. But not right now. First, we do the hard thing, and *then* we play."

"Hard thing," I giggled again. "I can do the hard thing. I'm open to that." My innuendo was lame, and Liam didn't do more than smile.

"C'mon. Focus."

He rose again, and I tried to calm my mind down enough to listen to the scripted apology this time. The frustrating thing—aside from the fact that it was keeping me from kissing Liam more—was that I didn't know how to act on camera. I'd inherited none of my father's talent that had made him so famous. Plus, after the mixed messages from Mom and Dad about tears while reading the apology, I wasn't sure what I was supposed to do or how I was supposed to behave. Welcome to the entirety of my childhood.

Liam told me I could cry or not cry, whatever felt real in the moment. What felt real right now was that I didn't want to deal with *any* of this. But I would because Liam was here with me, and he was going to help.

Currently, he was setting up the iPhone for me, getting the camera angle, so I was in the frame, but no hints could be found as to my location. "They'll get over being mad," he murmured, obviously talking about my parents. He fiddled with the various items from around the room we'd found to act as a sort of prop for the phone. "Eventually."

I combed a hand through my hair, wrecking it even more.

"Have you noticed, Liam? No one else has asked me if I'm okay. Not my parents, not Southerland. Just you."

Liam looked up, and I felt his gaze like a physical thing, a force that held me in its grasp. Like on *Star Wars.* "I'm sorry. They've always had the wrong priorities when it comes to you." He huffed a strange little laugh. "When it comes to *life*, for that matter."

"What do you think their priorities should be?"

"One hundred and eighty degrees different," Liam said, having turned his attention back to the task at hand. "There. We're ready."

"I'm not."

"I know, but the sooner this part is over, the sooner we can move on."

"Move on to kissing some more? And other stuff?"

Liam's eyes lifted again, and I could read the heat in them easily. "It's been a few years since we saw each other. Maybe we should take time to catch up before we hop in the sack."

"I don't want to," I said. "It's not like I'm going to want you less if we talk. It usually just makes me want you more."

Liam rounded from the setup and knelt in front of me, caressing my newly shaven cheek. I'd shaved while he'd read over the apology scripts and chosen one. I hadn't wanted to look like a total mess in the recording since it would exist forever on the internet—alongside my dick.

He murmured, "You really want me to be your first? You won't have regrets later?"

"Yes, and definitely not."

"I don't want to be accused of taking advantage of you during a rough time in your life. I couldn't resist earlier, but I should take better care of you. Make sure you're emotionally ready and—"

"I'm so ready," I said, putting my own hands on his cheeks and making him look at me. "I want you. I've always wanted you. I can't think of a better man to teach me everything I need to know."

"But surely you want some food first or—"

"Liam, please."

"Let's do this recording, and afterward, we'll talk about it more. I mean, you at least need some sleep. You must be tired."

I sighed and released his face. "Let's do the apology." As Liam went back behind the phone, I smoothed my hair down. "Do I look okay?"

"You look beautiful," he whispered, soft and encouraging. "You've got this. C'mon."

After he pressed record, I stumbled through the script that'd been prepared for me. It didn't sound smooth, but it was as real as possible when I was speaking the words someone else wrote for me—and lying. Still, when Liam and I watched it back, all my stumbling and near hyperventilating made me look sincerely horrified.

"That's because I am sincerely horrified," I said.

We sent the recording off to my folks' attorneys and sat holding hands and nuzzling each other's necks, kissing each other softly until we got a response saying it was "good enough," and then it was over.

Or as over it was ever going to be.

I expected to hear back from my family once it went live, but all I got was a thumbs up from Southerland and nothing at all from my parents. I remembered they had a Christmas charity auction to attend today. They were likely fielding questions about me right now. Even if they hadn't been as nice to me as I'd needed, I felt sorry for what I'd done to them and the way I'd ruined their holiday.

"Now," Liam said, coming around to kneel in front of me again. "Options: the inn offers romantic, snowy sleigh rides through the farm next door, or we can go on a walk around the lake, or we could sit on the back porch and look at the view."

I furrowed my brow. "Why do you keep trying to put off sex with me? Did I do it so wrong earlier you're not interested now?" I remembered he hadn't come.

"That's not it at all. I just...I feel...those three years I was guarding you, I felt like I had to push my feelings down, keep them back, and I worry if I let them loose now, I'll overwhelm you."

"Overwhelm me," I pleaded. "Please."

"But why not wait? Why not go downstairs and—"

"I'm never leaving this room again," I stated bluntly. "Everyone out there has seen my dick!"

He smiled, a rumble of a laugh in his throat. "North..."

"You can't even deny it."

"No, I can't."

"So, I'll just stay here until everyone forgets what I look like."

"That's impossible. You're too beautiful to forget."

"Ugh. I know."

He laughed again. "You're adorable, too."

"But I'm not leaving this room today," I said again.

"What about food?"

"Room service."

Liam twinkled at me like he had me now. "They don't have room service here."

"What?" I gasped. "What kind of place is this? Do they just leave their guests hungry?"

"They serve meals family-style three times a day."

"Great. I'm going to starve." I mourned, crossing my arms over my chest and rubbing my arms. "But I'm still not leaving." I brightened. "You'll bring me food, won't you? You won't let me go hungry."

Liam laughed, rolling his eyes. I loved how he even had freckles on his eyelids beneath his brows. He was so handsome and strongly built that it was easy to be distracted from what he said next just by thinking about all the things I liked about how he looked.

And there were even more things I liked about who he was as a person, too.

"Did you hear me?" he asked. "What about a drive into Sandpoint?"

"No."

"What if I wrap your head in a towel so that no one will see your face and smuggle you out to the lake?"

"Mm, maybe," I conceded. "But not today."

"You're set on this, aren't you?"

"Yes!" I exclaimed, coming to the end of my patience. "Why are you making me chase after you? After I waited for so many years?"

His expression slipped from amused to sad, and he rose to stand. "You're right. No more chasing. No more waiting. There's no reason to hold back now. You're twenty-one. You're not my boss. I'm not your bodyguard, and you've already agreed you're—" he smiled sweetly as he lifted his shirt and pulled it over his head, tossing it aside, "—my baby."

"Yeah, I'm your baby," I said, pulling my hoodie off and throwing it across the room. My heart pounded, my cock throbbed, and I felt dizzy. This was going to happen. He was going to do the stuff I'd only dreamed about. We were going to feel so good with each other. I knew it.

Liam jerked his jeans and underwear down. I did the same, kicking them off my feet just before he pushed me back on the bed and kissed me, making my bones turn to jelly and my pulse race in my ears.

The world wiped out around me until it was just his skin on my skin, his breath in my mouth, and his tongue against mine. I writhed, wanting more, wanting to merge our bodies and souls.

From somewhere in the B&B, there came the sound of a piano—"Santa Tell Me"—sliding through the room, just as Liam slid down my body, pushed my legs back, and put his mouth where no mouth had ever been.

I didn't know how he managed it because my dick was pretty long and thick, but somehow he took me in deep enough that I slid right into his throat. I cried out in shock when his swallow gripped and released me. I almost blew my load right then.

I gripped the sheets in one hand and shoved the other fist in my mouth, holding back a shout. Liam slid up until my cock left his throat, and I almost protested. But he started sucking and licking instead, and the sensation was so slick and tickly, so good and intense, I felt like I was rising out of my skin. "You like doing this?" I asked, embarrassment heating my cheeks.

Liam pulled off with a slurping sound, leaving my dick aching for his hot mouth again. "I love doing this."

I didn't have space to express any more of my embarrassment or fears, lost instead in the heat and suction, the ever-building, never-quite-breaking need that rose in me. Liam was amazing at giving head. He knew how to keep me on edge, pulling away to play with my balls or to kiss my inner thighs whenever I was about to explode.

"Please," I whispered. "I need it. I can't take it, Liam. Make me come."

Liam laughed and went back to making me twist and groan with need and pleasure.

He took me higher and higher and backed me back down again. Liam relented only when tears were standing in my eyes and I was gasping in near sobs. This time, thank God, he didn't back off when my balls drew up tight, instead sucking harder and taking me deeper. My fingers scrabbled against his scalp, and I strained toward my third orgasm with the man of my dreams. I needed it. I wanted it. I had to—

"Liam," I whimpered. "Oh, oh *God*!" I gripped his hair, and he sucked harder, moving his tongue relentlessly over the head of my dick. I arched, legs coming up around his shoulders as I shouted, "*Liam!*"

I exploded with pleasure, the intensity of my orgasm hitting like a strike of lightning. I groaned and tossed my head as he milked every drop of my bliss out of my dick and swallowed it down.

"Liam," I whined, teary and overcome.

He released me from his mouth and crawled up to cradle me in his arms. I was still jerking and shaking, mini strikes still clapping through me though my balls were drained.

"You're sweet, baby," he whispered. "You taste so good and sweet."

I groaned as he took hold of my chin and positioned my head for a kiss. The taste of my cum was harsh and familiar from my past curiosity-driven taste tests, but Liam's kiss made it as delicious as honey.

I melted as he passed the remnants of my jizz over to me. He sucked my lips and licked into my mouth until it was as red, tingly, and sensitive as my cock. Time stopped being real as Liam and I were swept away in each other.

As my chin began to burn from the friction, Liam pulled back. His chin and the area around his lips were lightly burned by my stubborn stubble, too.

"Ready for my dick?" he asked, panting and shoving his hard cock against my hip.

"Yes?" I whispered, wondering if he meant to fuck me.

But no. He lowered my legs and climbed over me, dropping kisses and licks along the way until he straddled my chest. After he placed some pillows beneath my head and I realized what he intended, my heart jolted, anxiety pinning me down.

"I've…I've never," I reminded him. His cock was beautiful. His average-sized shaft and cockhead, both smaller than mine, were much prettier than the mammoth dicks I'd seen in porn. I thought I could even fit a lot of it into my mouth. But what would I do with it once I did? How did I make it good for him?

"Just play with me," he encouraged. "You don't have to do anything more than have fun."

Liam's red pubic hair shimmered, and I ran my fingers through it, touching his soft sac and taking hold of his velvet, hard dick. The tip was red with urgency, and a drop of pre-cum rested there. I tasted it.

"Oh, North, yes," he murmured. "That's it. Make me feel good."

It didn't seem hard to please him, though I didn't think I was doing a great job. My lips stretched wide when he thrust deeper, almost making me gag, and I wondered how he could fit me into his mouth at all. I experimented with my tongue, and I touched his sac with awe. It felt a lot like my own, but knowing it was Liam's made everything about it thrilling, and when his balls drew up tight, I felt full of pride—I'd done this; I'd made Liam nearly come! I could have burst. But every time he got close, Liam pulled out to kneel over me, stroking his own cock, and staring down at me.

"North, you're so fucking beautiful. Jesus."

"You're beautiful, too," I said, my voice hoarse and shaky. "Come for me? I want to swallow your cum." I opened my mouth, begging with my eyes.

"Jesus fuck," he gritted out, gripping my jaw and jerking himself off faster and faster. "Open, baby, open up."

I opened as wide as I could with his fingers holding me in place, and when he flushed bright red all the way up to his hairline, I pushed my tongue forward, not wanting to miss any of his jizz.

"Here it comes," Liam moaned. "Swallow it. Fuck, oh, *fuck*, swallow it for me."

He threw his head back, his chest going redder than I'd ever

seen it, and his breath came in raging gasps. The spurts came fast
and hard. Desperately, I swallowed his load. It tasted like my own.
All baking soda-flavored and harsh. I loved it.

My eyes filled with tears. He was too gorgeous. I still couldn't
believe this was all real.

"North," he murmured before kissing me. "You're so sweet.
Damn."

"You're sweet, too," I whispered.

He slipped down again, and teasing kisses dropped down his
path. My legs trembled as he fell to sucking my cock again, and I
almost ascended into heaven as he showed me again how good he
was at it.

I gripped his hair, hips jerking up, and I groaned as I shook and
deposited my cum in his gulping throat. "Oh my God," I gasped.

The sounds of "O Holy Night" on the piano drifted up, and
Liam collapsed next to me, his eyes bright.

"Oh, holy baby," he whispered. "You're the best gift ever. Holy
fuck."

"If I'm a present, open me," I demanded. "Open me all the
way."

"Mmm."

"Fuck me," I begged. "Please, Liam."

Liam nuzzled my hair. "Your wish is my command. But not
today." He was still panting from sucking me off. "You need to rest.
It's been a long night and morning for you."

"But Liam—"

He pressed his fingers to my lips with a smile. "I promise it'll be
worth the wait. Trust me."

I wanted to argue, but I did trust him.

I waited it out, orgasm denied, until I surprised myself by falling
asleep. I dreamed Liam was sucking me off again, and dream-Liam
was just as good as real-Liam at deep throating. Dream-me shouted

as I came for him. I woke up in Liam's arms, panting and sticky. He woke and laughed at my predicament and the messy sheets.

"Luckily, I know where to get more," he said, peeling them off me. "You look awfully satisfied with yourself."

I grinned. I sure as hell was. Despite Liam's best efforts to make me wait, I'd still managed to get what I wanted. Post-orgasmic joy filled me, and I felt bone-deep satisfied in every way.

Stretching back as Liam got a warm washcloth to clean me up, I murmured, "Fourth orgasm."

"And to think the poor guy in the Partridge song only got four calling birds," Liam said, bending down to kiss me. "I'd say you're luckier."

"I'm ready to go for a fifth."

Liam laughed, tugged on the complimentary robe, and left the room for clean sheets, saying as he exited the door, "I'll see if I can find five golden rings instead. That seems just as likely to happen."

I didn't know what he meant, but I fell asleep before he returned and didn't wake up for hours.

CHAPTER EIGHT

Liam

AFTER I'D CLEANED him up after his wet dream—hopefully starring me—North had gone back to sleep, exhausted from four orgasms and the stressful night and morning. Drool slipped from the edge of his kiss-roughened mouth. I smiled fondly and nudged the blanket higher around his exposed chest, admiring the dark chest hair I'd tangled my fingers in and rubbed my balls against as we'd gotten off. More than that—made love.

I'd never felt that way about oral before, but with North? Hell, yes. Love. There was no denying it. I'd loved him for so long, and even with these past few years between us, we fit back together easily.

Nothing was awkward once we started talking, and nothing at all had been awkward in bed—well, for me, anyway. North had clearly found some of it embarrassing, but he'd come into his own.

It was everything I'd ever imagined, and it *finally* wasn't wrong anymore. I had every right to touch and be touched by him. Beautiful.

I'd slipped from bed after catching a quick nap. I showered and put on my clothes again, all while North dozed away. I figured he'd had a stressful night and would probably sleep for a while yet, but we'd already missed lunch, and dinner was still a few hours away. He always ate like a horse, and after the physical exertion we'd just put in, he'd be even hungrier.

After writing a note on the little Christmas tree-shaped pad left in the room, along with a candy cane-shaped pen, I slipped out into the hallway and made my way toward the stairs.

As I passed Room Nine, the door opened, and a handsome gentleman poked his head out, caught my eye, and thrust several rolls of toilet paper into my hands before shutting the door behind him again.

I blinked in confusion and considered knocking to ask what was going on but decided against it. If the guy didn't want the toilet paper, he didn't want the toilet paper. "Why" didn't really matter. Maybe he'd brought his own? And as for why he gave it to me, maybe I'd retained the air of an employee here? It didn't matter. Life was weird, and some things in it didn't get explanations.

I added the rolls of toilet paper to the stack of them in the cleaning closet at the end of the hallway, as well as grabbed some lube from the complimentary stash of sex supplies provided to guests upon request. Oh, how awkward it would have been to make that request of my second mother, though. I was glad I knew where the gratis items were stored, and I didn't have to.

Retreating with what I needed concealed in my pockets, I took the stairs down to the first floor to get sandwiches. I gave Sal a thumbs-up and a smile as I passed by the reception desk and into the dining room. Thankfully he was busy with Blustery Bill Lawson—the local weatherman and his husband had been annual guests here at Christmastime, even back when I worked here. I was able to escape without having to dodge his certain thirst for gossip about North.

Once I'd passed through the door from the dining room into the kitchen, my own hunger hit me. The scents of a slow-roasting turkey and other yummy items being prepared for dinner made my mouth water and stomach rumble.

"Well, look who came to visit," Suzanne said with a smile, her hands floury from making pie crusts for the evening's dessert selection.

I smiled at her and crossed the kitchen to give her a peck on the cheek. Normally she wouldn't be alone in here working. Jerome was her right-hand man, and he did a lot of the prep work for her.

"Where's Jerome?" I asked.

"Had to run to town to buy more cinnamon for the sweet potato casseroles. Can you believe I let us run out? At Christmas!"

I shook my head. "You must have had something else on your mind."

"Not really. It's been busy around here, but no more than usual."

I cocked my hip and leaned against the counter. "You don't seem surprised to see me."

"Rumor had it you were here."

I laughed. "Oh, yeah, and what did you hear?"

"That the famous young man you used to bodyguard—" she paused. "Is that a verb?"

"Protect," I supplied.

"Yes. Well, Sal blabbed, as usual, and told us the boy is upstairs hiding out after a rough time, and *then* he said you'd come here to lure him out."

"That about sums it up," I agreed.

"Any luck?"

I snorted. "None at all. He's determined he's going to take over the room indefinitely, possibly for the rest of his life, and he'll just pay extra to have someone deliver his meals to the door."

Suzanne chuckled. "Poor kid."

"My thoughts exactly."

"I hear the rest of the world is being pretty hard on him."

"Including his parents."

"Did they hire you to find him?"

I shook my head.

Suzanne gave me a thoughtful glance. "And what brought him here to our Camp Bay Chalet? I can't imagine he was just passing by when his—ahem—broke the internet."

"Have you been on Twitter, Suz? 'Broke the internet.' Next thing you know, you'll be posting selfies from the kitchen with, 'Not me making a delicious dinner for Camp Bay Chalet guests.'"

"I'm not ready to be old yet! I've got to learn the slang to stay young, and you're not far off. Jerome wants us to be more active on our social media pages for the Chalet."

Strong footsteps interrupted us, and I turned, smiling, already knowing who it belonged to.

"Ah, I was wondering if you were ever going to come out of that room," Rhonda said. A very waggy Molly was at her side.

Molly darted over to me, her tongue lolling in joy as she jumped at my legs and wriggled in joyous circles. I squatted down next to her, scrubbing her soft ears and letting her press against me.

"Did you miss me, girl?" I asked.

"You shouldn't be such a stranger. It weighs on Molly's mind when she doesn't see you," Rhonda said, though I knew when she said "Molly," she meant herself. After giving me a hug, she put her hands on her hips and said, "Speaking of strangers, that boy up there? He's doing okay? I don't want my Christmas guests disturbed by some dramatic incident that requires me to call the police. No tragedy, just joy, you get my drift?"

"He's going to be fine," I said. "I guess you know what happened?"

"Dollface, the whole world knows what happened."

"You can imagine how humiliated he is right now." I went back to leaning on the counter.

She sighed, shaking her head sadly. "The apology he posted is already making the rounds."

"A famous apology, filmed in our guest room," Suzanne murmured.

I asked, "And how's it going over?"

"From what I've overhead from the gossipier of our guests, pretty well." Rhonda winked.

"Some believe him, and some don't, right?"

"More don't than do, but it doesn't matter because the kid was sad-looking and adorable; I think everyone with a heart is going to forgive him."

"I hope so. But more importantly, I hope he can forgive himself."

"Exactly!" Rhonda exclaimed. "It's Christmas. He should be home with his family. I take it they aren't allowing him to come?" She tsked. "Family…what good are they?"

I shrugged.

I'd never struggled with family the way Rhonda and Suzanne had. My mom and dad had accepted me when I came out, but, more importantly, even if they hadn't, I'd already created a second home here at Camp Bay Chalet, and I'd known I could depend on them for support even if worse came to worst.

Rhonda and Suzanne, though, had been disowned by their families over their love. Rhonda was the most bitter about it, but only because she loved Suzanne so much; she was offended by anyone on earth not loving her too. And that included both their families.

"I think he chose not to go home on his own accord," I said, pulling out a stool and having a seat. My legs were still feeling shaky after the orgasm from earlier. Weird how sexual exertion could have effects pure exercise didn't. Right now, I felt like I could've run a marathon and ended it with less residual shakiness and rushing endorphins. "His family is…complicated."

"I was just asking Liam before you came in what brought this young man to Camp Bay," Suzanne said. "With his wealth, I'd have thought he'd want to hide out in, I don't know, Cabo San Lucas or wherever the new hotspot is for the rich and famous."

"Isn't it Puerto Vallarta again?" Rhonda asked. "I feel like I'm hearing a lot about Puerto Vallarta."

"He came because of me."

Suzanne and Rhonda exchanged a knowing glance. "I thought so."

"He and I..." I cleared my throat, heat burning my cheeks. "Never did anything when I was his bodyguard. I was his employee, and—"

Suzanne lifted her floury hands from shaping the corners of the pies. "You don't have to defend yourself to us, sweetpea. We've known you most of your life, and we know you're an honorable man."

"A lot of men are 'honorable' until they're faced with temptation," I said. "It's not like it wasn't a strain. I'm ashamed to say it, but I was half in love with him when he wasn't even eighteen yet. He didn't know, of course. I never told him anything inappropriate, but it was wrong to feel that way."

"Wrong? You were a baby yourself."

"Yes, but—"

"Whatever. You didn't touch him or groom him. There's no crime in wanting to do something," Rhonda said. "The crime is in the doing."

Suzanne blew Rhonda a kiss. "Exactly. Go on, Liam."

"By the time he fired me, I was head over heels for him, and he did the right thing to let me go. He was legal but still too young. Neither of us were ready."

"And now he's old enough *and* ready?"

Heat flamed in my cheeks again. "He's old enough. I don't know about ready. He's young still—"

"So are you!"

"—and sheltered in his own way. He's also..." How did I describe this without sounding like North was somehow less than he really was? "He's naïve, trusts too easily, and doesn't think things through. I want to help him. If we also have more, so be it."

"Tell me more about this boy," Suzanne said, taking one pie over to the oven and sliding it in.

"He's kind," I said. "And he never means to make mistakes; he just makes them accidentally with his whole, pure heart. He's funny without trying, anxious, though..." I paused, remembering. "And the first time I ever saw him, something in me just lit up inside, like he'd flipped a switch in me just by existing."

"Love at first sight?"

"Not that I could admit to myself at the time," I clarified. "But from the safety of the years between now and then and being out of the dangerous predicament of being attracted to my too-young protectee, I can say, yeah. It was love at first sight for me."

"What about for him?"

"I don't know the answer to that," I said. "I've never asked."

Of course, I hadn't. It was only just today we'd even admitted all of this to each other—and consummated the feelings that had been burning inside us both for way too long.

"What's your goal? To get him out of that room and take him home to your mama as a Christmas present?"

I grinned. "I'd sure like that, but right now, I just want to take him a sandwich or two."

Rhonda nodded and went to the big refrigerator, pulling out the tray with the leftover sandwiches from lunch. She set about putting together plates of food for us both. The sandwiches were joined by mixed fruit and four iced Christmas cookies.

As she worked, I went on, "He's ashamed and afraid of the other guests in the hotel. He's convinced everyone will instantly recognize him, and he doesn't want to have to stand there knowing whoever he's talking to has seen his—err, you know."

"Gigglestick? Shaft of delight? Flesh flute?" Suzanne said, her sweet face breaking into a smile as words that didn't match her motherly face casually fell from her lips.

"Yup," I said, laughing and plucking an extra cookie from the tray before Rhonda turned to put it back in the fridge. Rhonda playfully slapped my hand and went to prepare a cup of hot chocolate for me just the way I liked it. The feeling of home swept over me as I'd never left working here.

"Most of the guests for the weekend are either too self-absorbed to care about something like North's pole, or they'll be delighted to know the owner of that monster."

I almost choked on my cookie, crumbs sucking down my throat. I coughed inelegantly until Rhonda pounded my back.

"I might be a lesbian, but I know a big one when I see it."

"Christ," I muttered. "Warn a guy before saying something like that about his boyfriend's—" I broke off, both because I didn't want to say 'dick' in front of them and because I'd just called North my boyfriend. I sure as hell hoped he was.

"Your boyfriend," Suzanne said, another grin crinkling her eyes. "I like the sound of that."

"Super wealthy, super handsome, super *other things*," Rhonda's eyes twinkled. "I like the sound of it for him, too."

I groaned.

"We want to meet him," Suzanne said. "How are you going to get him out of the room?"

"I just need to come up with a plan that works. I tried earlier but failed." Maybe I'd have some success now our mutual need had cooled. "Who's here this year?"

Sometimes celebrities and athletes were guests for Christmas. The Chalet had a reputation as a high-class, cozy place for the upper crust who craved a more downhome experience to spend their holidays.

If there were someone in the group North would want to meet, like a Formula 1 racer or a member of a band he liked, he might be intrigued enough to come out. Even if he had to endure knowing whoever it was had seen his cock. Maybe.

"Oh, no one too famous this year. Except for North."

I rolled my eyes.

"Let's see," Suzanne said, her eyes casting upward as she searched her mind for the guest list. "We've got..." She ran through a list as long as it was varied—which is to say moderately long. The main guests of interest for me were Pierce Hunter, of the ghost-hunting TV show fame, and his boyfriend Haven, a horror author. "The couple from Tennessee—Walker Ronson and Ashton Sellers—are adorable, and so are Pierce and Haven. Pierce is quite famous now, isn't he? Then there's Max—"

Rhonda and Suzanne shared a mutual, hopeful look before Suzanne went on to finish the list with Blustery Bill, the weatherman, and Agatha Sanders, psychologist to the stars.

"Maybe Agatha could help North?" Suzanne said, eyes brightening. "I'm sure he could afford her fee."

"She's on vacation," Rhonda warned. "I'm sure she doesn't want to work, and it wouldn't be right to ask her."

"No," I agreed. "Besides, North has an aversion to psychologists ever since his parents made him go to one for some constipation issues he was having at the time. They'd decided it was all in his head." I rolled my eyes.

"Wow."

"That's what they're like."

"Poor kid. But if Agatha just happens to talk with him?"

"Don't try to arrange anything," Rhonda warned. "You know what happens when you meddle."

My phone buzzed, and I snatched it from my pocket, expecting it to be North calling to ask how much longer I'd be with the food. But the face filling the screen of the FaceTime call was decidedly not North's.

I raised a hand to Rhonda and Suzanne, indicating I'd need to take the call, and they both fell quiet.

"Hey, kiddo," I said, smiling into the phone. Aiden's face weaved around the screen.

"When you comin' home?" he asked. "I miss youuuuu."

"Oh, for heaven's sake, Aiden, who have you called?" My mom's voice sounded both amused and exasperated as she took the phone from Aiden's hand. Rhonda and Suzanne both chuckled quietly. "Oh, thank God it's just you. I was afraid it was another call to 911."

"I think he learned after the last time."

"The fireman was mean to me!" Aiden cried from somewhere in the kitchen where he'd started opening and shutting cupboards by the sound of it.

Mom looked harried, pushing her frizzy red hair out of her face, and heaving a sigh, she said, "I hate to ask, but when will you be home? This one's got all the energy of a freight train, and his mama is…" she lifted her voice higher, like she was saying something nice, "…out meeting up with her attorney to finalize the custody arrangement changes for next year."

"Well, I hate to break it to you, but I might not be home today at all. Or tonight, either."

"What? Why?" Mom bent low, causing the scene on the screen to swoop. There were the sounds of a little tussle before she reappeared again with a spoon covered in Nutella. "That's not for eating out of the jar, young man. It's for spreading on bread and toast."

"I'b not a yun' man," Aiden said, his mouth clearly full of the hazelnut and chocolatey goodness. "I'b a baby."

91

"You're a toddler, and—"

"No! I'b a baby!"

She sighed. "He's in one of his moods. He's annoyed because I've been holding Jack while he slept, and—" There was a thump and a howling sound in the background. "Dammit. Jack just rolled off the couch. Here, take this, Aiden."

She thrust the Nutella spoon back at him, to his loud delight. "I need to check on him." The wailing got louder as she hustled to the living room. "Shh, Gammy's here. I have you." The tears and snuffles continued for a moment before Jack's curious face appeared on the screen.

"Hi, little bub," I said. "You're okay."

He turned to cuddle up against my mom again, quiet and solemn, as only Jack could be before he got up his energy to wreak baby havoc. It was unfortunate for my mom Aiden was also having a rough day. I knew it was hard to keep up with them both at her age. Still, I wasn't going home.

"You can handle them until Maeve gets home, Mom. I believe in you." I raised a fist so she could see me cheer her on. "You've got this. You raised Maeve and me, after all."

"You two were angels."

"So are these sweet monsters."

She snorted. "Sweet angel-monsters, that's about right." She tilted her head, taking in the background of where I was. "I see you're at Camp Bay. I assume you're planning to stay there."

I nodded.

"But I also know they're all booked up this time of year, so who's keeping you away from home tonight?"

"North."

She continued to rock and pat Jack's back, but her lips went tight. "Your North?"

"Yeah."

Mom gave a heavy sigh and another, heavier sigh as she said, "Aiden, don't just eat it from the…okay, fine. That's your jar, though. No one else's."

"Yay!" he cried.

"North, huh?" Mom said, coming back to me.

"Yeah."

I expected her to remind me of how North had fired me in the middle of a pandemic, the way Maeve always did when he came up. Instead, she said, "Well, all right. But I want to meet him. Bring him home with you."

"I don't know about that. And I don't know when I'll be home."

"For Christmas at least?" she asked. "I'd hoped when you lost that job, you'd stop having reasons to spend Christmas away from home."

"Hopefully, for Christmas," I agreed.

"Good."

"Oh, and Mom?"

"Yes?"

"Can you do a favor for me? Go into my room and pack a bag with some more clothes. A few days' worth. Sweaters, jeans, enough for both North and me. I'm going to text Jerome and ask him to swing by and pick it all up from you. He's in town buying cinnamon for Suzanne."

Mom agreed though I wondered if I'd find a half-eaten container of Nutella and a stowaway child inside instead of clothes when I opened my bag.

"Oh, and Mom? Please. For the love of God. Don't look North up on the internet right now."

"Oh?"

"Yeah, I'll explain later, or Maeve will. Just promise."

"I don't think I'll have time to check FaceSpace with these

two—" Jack started squirming to be let down, and Mom obliged. "Don't smear that on—" She sat Jack on the ground and said, "Liam, honey, just bring the boy home. Besides, I've already seen his honky-honk. It's too late to protect me from *that*. My friend Mary Beth is passing it all around our group chats."

"What?" I cried. "Why would she do that?"

"She claims to have slept with the boy's grandfather, the hotelier, once years ago when she was trying to make it as a star in Hollywood. She said North appears to have inherited at least one thing from the man."

"That's…" I sputtered.

Aiden shouted, Jack screamed, and Mom said, "Have to go. Love you. Bye."

Turning away from my phone and back to the room, Rhonda and Suzanne burst out laughing.

"Don't you even," I said, shaking a warning finger at them.

I texted Jerome and hoped he got the message in time.

If North and I were going to stay here a few more days, we'd both soon be in desperate need of fresh clothes.

CHAPTER NINE
North

how's the weather? I texted Southerland using our code words for checking on the temperature of the family—were things still hot, cooling off, or wet and weepy, that sort of thing.

there's a cool breeze blowing in, and the storm clouds have passed over. good job with the apology

thanks. i'm wondering what you think would happen if i just don't come home for christmas

honestly? they'd probably be relieved if you didn't. everything is still really awkward right now, and they still have four more parties before the end of the year, and those are just the ones they're hosting

are they making you go to them all?

i told them if they even try to make me go anywhere this year, i'll embarrass them even worse than you did. they believed me

I wasn't surprised. Southerland had been making it clear for several years now she hated the holiday whirlwind, and my mistake had put fear in their hearts. Southerland was using that to her advantage. Smart girl.

what about the parties at home?

pj party alone in my room. the east rooms will be off-limits to guests

sounds great

come home, and you can party with me, or don't come home but tell me your plans. did you and Liam…

She sent through a purple devil-horn emoji.

I replied: *and if we did?*

ugh. you'll be spending the holidays with him?

yeah, maybe. i don't know. we haven't discussed it. but even if he doesn't want to or can't, i don't want to go home. i'd rather stay right here. i haven't actually left my room, but so far, this chalet is pretty chill.

There was a longer-than-usual pause before Southerland replied, *what do you want from Liam?*

I didn't know how to answer, and luckily she didn't make me. The bubble appeared, indicating she was typing again. I let it come through instead of trying to figure out what to say. How did I know what I wanted from him? We'd just found each other again. I mean, ideally, we'd fall fully in love and get married and adopt puppies and stay together forever. But what did I know about that?

he's a great guy, but make sure you're both on the same page. it would suck if you were thinking this is some great romance while he's thinking it's a short-term fling to get his rocks off with the guy he wanted so bad a few years ago

The comment stung more than I thought it should. Why wouldn't Liam want me for more than that? I might not be the smartest guy he'd ever met, but I was a good person, he'd said so himself, and earlier, when he'd been holding me, making me feel good, his eyes had said this was anything but a fling. But what if I was wrong? I was wrong a lot.

Southerland didn't seem to require a reply, so I ditched the conversation to open my other unread texts and started replying to each one by one. People being assholes about the pic got a middle finger emoji. People being kind got a blows-kiss emoji. People asking questions about what happened got a 'more later,' and, if I really liked the person, a heart. But, again, no one asked if I was okay or how I felt. I needed better friends and people in my life.

I'd just reached the last text when my phone lit up with an incoming call. *Grandma Ford* flashed on my screen, and my stomach flipped anxiously. She was the easy grandmother. The one who didn't care more about what the rest of the world thought than about me, but still—she'd seen my dick!

I answered reluctantly. "Hi, Grandma."

"Hey, sweetie," she said in her smooth Southern-accented tones. "I've been worried about you."

"I'm sorry. I screwed up."

"I wish I was there to give you a big hug."

I sighed, tears in my eyes. "Thank you, Grandma." I sat up straighter. "How are things there? Southerland seems to think it's calmer now."

"A lot less shouting. Merlina has stopped lecturing your parents about how they missed their chance by not sending you to military school when you were younger."

"Grandma Astor always thought I'd do well in a military academy."

"Perhaps, but I think you're a wonderful young man just the way you are. Your heart is always in the right place."

My heart. That was a part of my body everyone loved to talk about—well, and now my dick—because my brain wasn't "always in the right place."

"I won't be home for Christmas," I said, without acknowledging the rest of what she'd said. I liked having a good heart, but I wished I was smarter, too. I wished I had what it took to be a lawyer, doctor, or astronaut even. Not because I found any of those jobs interesting, but because people wouldn't say things like, "North has such a good heart" in that pitying sort of way. And if I were smart enough to be one of those things, I'd be smart enough to find them interesting, too, right?

"Your father says you're with your old bodyguard Liam, and Merlina implied you and he were, well, perhaps *involved*," Grandma ventured. "Is he…I mean, I know there was a picture of you kissing a boy at a Halloween party not long ago, but I was never sure… You know I love you no matter what you do or say or are, right? Or who you love?"

I blinked, confused. Didn't everyone know I liked guys and

girls? I felt like that'd been obvious from the start, but I went ahead and answered her. "I'm here with Liam, and yeah, we're…" I paused. I couldn't say we were dating. I couldn't say he was my boyfriend, could I? Maybe he was?

"Involved?" Grandma Ford offered again.

"Yeah, and I think I'm going to spend Christmas here with him. It'll be better for everyone that way."

"Well, I'll miss seeing your face, but if you're happy in the company of this young man, I'm happy for you. I know you've been through a lot these last few days, and I hope he's comforting you well."

"He is."

"Would you like me to pass on this news to your parents? Or will you call them yourself?"

"You tell them, please. I don't want to get another lecture from them about anything, whether it's staying here for Christmas or more yelling about what a big mistake I made with…with the, uh, picture."

"All right. I want you to know, sweetie, there's nothing you could ever do to make me not love you. Just in case you were worried about that."

"I know," I whispered.

"You're my sweet boy."

"I love you, Grandma."

"Now enjoy your time with your friend, and I'll let your parents know you won't be coming for Christmas."

"They'll probably be happier without me around," I said, awash in sudden self-pity.

"I don't know about that. They love you and were looking forward to seeing you. But you how they complicate things with worries about reputation and such." She tutted. "But this will all blow over. Scandals like these are a dime a dozen. Soon enough, someone else's mishap will be trending—is that the right word for it?"

"Yes."

"I'm learning your newfangled words."

Saying goodbye to her, my heart trembled.

Was I still trending? I was tempted to check. My finger hovered over the Twitter app symbol on my phone when the key sounded in the door.

I tossed my phone aside as Liam entered carrying a tray with plates on it. I sat up, about to climb out of bed to help him with it, when he stopped mid-stride and said, "Damn, you look good all naked in bed. Stay there. Don't move. Let me see you."

I did as he asked.

After he put the tray down on the small table, he turned back to me, crossed his arms over his chest, and took me in. "Screw sandwiches. *You* look good enough to eat," he smirked. "Again."

"Go on," I agreed. Liam's tongue on my cock had been a holiday miracle, and I was happy to have more of it.

"Later," he said, motioning toward the trays. "Let's eat real food instead. Fuel up for more fun later."

While Liam disappeared into the bathroom to wash his hands, I sat at the table and started in on the sandwich—thick bread with fixings and a finger's width of meat—and the cookies—iced in green, red, and white. They looked like the sugar cookies my favorite cook used to make to celebrate the holidays when Southerland and I were kids. Even if the recipe wasn't the same, they were wonderful.

"Yes, dig in," Liam encouraged, sitting down opposite me and taking a big bite of his sandwich. His eyes fell closed, his chestnut eyelashes shadowed his freckled cheekbones as he groaned. "So good. Suzanne puts something illegal in these sandwiches, I swear. I'm not sure what exactly, but I've never tasted better."

I took a bite of mine, and as the taste burst all over my mouth, making me groan, too, I said, "It's the mustard. Our cook before last used this mustard. It's the best."

"Cook before last," Liam murmured and chuckled. "Your family lives in a whole other world, North. You know that, right?"

I nodded. "Yeah, but what can I do about it? And, I guess, embarrassing as it is, I wouldn't know how to live any other way."

"I know," Liam said thoughtfully.

My phone buzzed, and Liam and I both turned toward it.

"It might be my parents," I admitted. "I talked to Grandma Ford earlier and told her I wouldn't be home for Christmas. I want to avoid all the parties and attention."

"And your parents want that?"

I nodded. "Well, Southerland says so. I haven't talked to them since you, and I did together."

"They haven't even texted?"

I shook my head.

"Damn. They're…they're something else."

"I know." I reached for the phone and, sure enough, it was a text from my mom.

Grandma Ford told us you're not coming for Christmas. Your dad and I will miss you this year. Despite the troubles going on, we want you to know we love you very much. Enjoy Christmas with Liam. It's a relief to know he'll take good care of you. We'll see you for Spring Break.

I read it aloud to Liam. "Don't worry. You're not stuck with me. I mean, obviously, you have to spend Christmas with your family and all. I'll just stay here at the chalet. They have activities, right? If I ever decide to leave the room." I snagged a second cookie and ate bites of it in between bites of sandwich. "I might just stay in and rewatch *Elf.* It'll be just like at home: a party downstairs and me alone with Buddy Elf."

"Your parents' life is something I don't think I could ever attempt to live."

"Yeah."

"You were raised in it. It must seem normal to you."

"I guess. But I'm willing to learn to have a different kind of life." I watched Liam's expression, suddenly worried he might be thinking I was too different from him. "Your kind of life."

Liam's lips tilted up at the edges. "How about we try to meet somewhere in the middle? I admit, after spending those years around your family, I can't say I envy them even a little for their fame or wealth, not when it comes with all those headaches."

"My dad had to deal with another stalker last month," I said, nodding. "It's so common now, Southerland and I don't even blink. Mom has her own issues. There's always some member of one of her clubs who's backstabbing her or gossiping about her or trying to seduce Dad."

"I remember."

"It's exhausting."

"How would you prefer to spend your life? What do you think is the perfect ordinary day?"

"For everyone?"

"Just for you. Like if you could imagine your ideal ordinary day."

"Hmm. I'm not sure." I chewed my sandwich and gazed out of the window. "I like painting these days. I've started putting my dragons and aliens on bigger canvases now that I'm in Seattle and Mom can't complain about the smell of the paint."

"Yeah? Inside your apartment?"

I nodded. "I have a spare room, and I just put a drop cloth down and go to town in there. The canvases are huge, too." He paused. "If they were any bigger, I couldn't get them back out, and the ceilings are super high."

"So ideally, you'd paint all day?"

"I don't think I could do it all day. There's only so much time you can spend thinking about dragons and new designs for the wings."

Liam grinned. "You could paint other things."

"Maybe." I shifted slightly, embarrassment creeping in. "Okay, this is embarrassing to admit, but I trust you."

"Hit me."

"I like the idea of gardening."

"Like growing tomatoes and cucumbers?"

North shook his head. "No, like having a huge park-like area and laying out a big design that I make come to life with flowers and bushes and stuff. Maybe a dragon-shaped garden, but it'd be so big you could only see the dragon's colors from the air."

"What's keeping you from doing it? If it's education, I'm sure we could locate a program that can help you learn about horticulture and start working on smaller versions of this dream."

I shrugged. "It's awkward."

"Tell me anyway."

"I just did. Wanting to garden is weird. What's a guy like me doing with a dream like that? I'm supposed to dream bigger."

"What's a better dream for you?"

"Dad thinks I could act."

Liam lifted his brows as if to say 'seriously?' and I chuckled.

"I know, right? I can't act my way out of a paper bag, as Southerland says. Just think about how bad that apology would've been if I hadn't meant every word of it. Mostly."

"And what does Grandma Astor think you should do?"

"Model. She says I'm handsome enough for it. It's something a child of an actor can easily get a start in, and she says it's what pretty people do when they don't have the superior brains to match their superior face."

"Pardon me, but she's a bitch."

"Yeah, she is. Grandma Ford says I should write children's books? About dragons?" I sighed. "And it's not like it's a bad idea, but dragons aren't just for kids, you know?"

"I get it."

"Right now, I'm happy with what I'm doing with the big dragon paintings."

"Who have you told about this garden idea?"

I listed off some of the acquaintances in college I'd mentioned it to in passing. "They'd all stared at me like I'd said I dreamed of doing porn for a living. No, they probably would have stared *less* at that because they'd like to see me naked. Most of them would, anyway."

"I'd rather if only I saw you naked," Liam said, taking my hand. "I'm not the jealous type, but I'm the loyal type."

I liked that. It made me feel all wriggly and giddy inside. "Me too."

Though I was *also* the jealous type.

"Good."

"I've never told anyone in my family about the garden idea. I don't think they'd get it."

"Grandma Ford might."

I shook my head. "It's silly. I should forget about it."

"No, no," Liam said. "This is great stuff. It's not impossible to achieve, North. I think you could do it. I really do."

I appreciated his belief in me, but I didn't know where to even begin with it all. "I guess it doesn't matter, though, since I'm never leaving this room again."

"About that. This place is like my second home. The people here are good people. I promise it's safe to come out of this room."

"The people who work here, maybe, but what about the guests?"

"I know most of them, too, but even the ones I don't know, I feel certain they'd be kind to you."

"They've seen my dick," I murmured, feeling the sandwich start to come back up. "They'll know."

"Baby, I'm sorry this has happened to you, but staying in this room forever isn't the answer. This is a great place to practice pretending not to care about all this whenever you meet someone in the future. There are limited people here, and not one of them is going to be a jerk to you."

"It's humiliating."

"It is," Liam agreed. "But I'll be there with you, and we'll get you through it."

I cleared my throat. "Maybe. But later."

"Of course, later."

"I want to forget all about it for the rest of the night. Can we do that?"

"Sure. No phones, no internet. We'll stay in our room, and I'll have Rhonda bring up dinner."

"I thought you said they won't do that."

"I have an in with her," Liam teased. "She'll do it for me."

"Just for tonight?"

"Yeah. Tomorrow we'll take a step into facing the world again."

"No phones or internet tomorrow either?" I asked hopefully.

"If you leave the room with me, yes."

"All right. It's a deal."

After that, we finished our cookies, and I got down on my knees, gave Liam the sweetest look I could muster, and asked, "Can I suck your dick again? I really want to practice. I swear I can get good at it."

Liam touched my cheek. "You're welcome to use my dick to practice whenever you want. Seeing your mouth around me—" he shuddered. "It's fucking hot."

"Unzip your pants," I panted. "I want to suck you."

He did, and I did.

And for those moments, I forget everything but the scent of his crotch, the taste of his cum, and the sounds he made as I worked him over.

CHAPTER TEN

Liam

NORTH WASN'T GOD'S gift to blow jobs, but his enthusiasm had my legs shaking, my hips twitching, and my balls drawing up well before I wanted to come.

I needed it to last because it still seemed like a dream that North was with me, touching and being touched by me, and his lips were cherry red from being stretched around my girth.

"That's good," I praised him, smoothing a hand into his hair and holding him in place as I fucked into his mouth, taking control of the slick, wet friction. "You're so pretty. Look at you."

He groaned, and I decided coming in his mouth wasn't good enough. I yearned to paint him with my cum, rub it into his skin, and make him mine all over. He'd stink of me, and I'd coax his load out and add it to mine. A mixture of us on his body.

I pulled away from his mouth, and he came after me, mouth open like a baby bird hungry for more. "That's all for now," I said, lifting him to his feet and pushing him back on the bed. "Get that robe off. Get on your back."

He did as he was told, and I knelt between his splayed legs, gazing at his flushed cheeks, his red lips, and his hungry eyes, skimming my gaze over his hairy chest to where his cock beat with his pulse against his black pubes and taut belly. "You want to be mine, baby?"

"Yes."

"Want my jizz all over you?"

"Want it *in* me."

"Mm, yeah, I want that, too." I gritted my teeth against the temptation of pushing his legs back and thrusting into him without working up to it the way he needed. "But later."

North nodded, his pupils dilated, his cock leaking pre-come.

"Pinch your own nipples," I whispered. "I want to see it."

North's flush grew deeper, but he did as I asked, and when he started pinching them harder and harder with the rhythm of my hand flying over my aching cock, I felt the tension in me draw too tight to withstand.

I burst into orgasm with a shout and a sharp, hard jet of cum which took my breath away. The slick, white pearly stuff landed on his belly and chest, and I aimed my final load at his cock, unloading onto him.

As he pinched his nipples, I went down on his dick, cleaning up my cum and sucking him into my throat. He arched and nearly shot his load, but I pulled off again.

Reaching for the lube on the nightstand, I asked, "Want to be inside me? Don't worry. I'll control the whole thing. I'll show you how."

North shook his head, and I smiled. "That's okay, baby. It's good to say no when you don't want something." I put the lube back. "Besides, I'm probably too sensitive after that orgasm. My eyes might be bigger than my appetite in the end."

"Can I come?" North asked, voice shaky.

I cocked my head. "Asking permission?"

He nodded.

"All right. Hold on." I shifted, so I was poised over him, a hand on his throat, not hard at all, but gentle and reassuring, like I was keeping him safe. "Now, jerk yourself off. I'm going to watch your face when you come."

He whimpered, and a glimmer of insecurity shimmered in his

eyes, but he gamely took up his own dick, and as I took in every nuance of his twisting expression, his eyes screwing closed and opening again to watch me watching, I knew the moment he was going to break apart. It was gorgeous. Just like him.

His chest heaved as his cum jolted out of him in hard bursts, which left him shaking, whimpering. Sweet Jesus, it was hot.

North collapsed back on the bed, panting, and exhausted again. His eyes drooped as I rubbed our combined cum all over his skin, whispering about how he was mine now and he belonged to me.

"It's good to belong to someone," he slurred as he drifted off in post-coital sleep. "Never belonged to anyone like this before."

I collapsed on the mattress next to him and pulled him close. Kissing his hair, his neck, and his shoulder, I murmured, "Me either, baby. Me either."

CHAPTER ELEVEN
Liam

December 23

T HE NEXT MORNING, I rose before North, showered, and put on some of the fresh clothes my mom had packed and Jerome had delivered to our door last night. It was good to have on a new pair of jeans and to shave—she'd also tucked a razor, toothbrush, a tube of lube, and an entire box of condoms into the bag.

That was a little embarrassing—and unnecessary.

But thoughtful all the same.

I supposed she knew more than I'd realized about my feelings for North.

Careful not to wake my sleeping angel, I left the room and headed down to collect a late lunch. Again, I was abruptly stopped in the hall by the same man who'd given me the rolls of toilet paper the day before.

With sparking, mischievous eyes, he thrust an empty coffee pot my way, saying, "Get rid of this for me." Once I'd taken it from him, he strolled away, back to room nine.

Shaking my head, I carried the coffee pot with me to the elevator. While waiting for it to arrive, my phone buzzed with a text message.

Expecting it to be Maeve complaining I wasn't watching her kids, and thus making her life harder while I was wasting my time on a selfish kid who'd let me go during a pandemic and all the usual jazz, I was surprised to see the name on the screen.

Though I really shouldn't have been. I knew she cared about North.

"Eleesha," I said, taking the call and refusing the elevator when it arrived. Cell connection died in the tin can of it instantly. I walked to the end of the hallway with the window facing the lake. "How are you? I guess you saw."

"I did. And I also saw he's at some Chalet near you and—"

"You still have him on Find My iPhone?"

"Of course. Don't you? If anyone's in danger of getting lost out in the woods or something, it's our friend North. The more folks who can search him up, the merrier, I say."

"That's why you never removed my permissions on the app?"

"That, and I knew you'd want to keep tabs on him. It's not like it wasn't immediately obvious when I started protecting North what was going on between you guys."

"Nothing went on."

"I know. Because he fired you. His parents explained it to me when I approached them to ask if everything had been kosher."

"Thanks for trusting me," I scoffed.

"Hey, nice guys can be problematic, too." She sniffed. "So you don't seem surprised to hear he's at a chalet near you. I assume you're with him?"

The hint of accusation in her voice let me know what she thought I was doing with North, and the fact it was true pricked my conscience. "He can go where he wants to go and be who he wants to be with. He's grown now."

"I saw how grown he is on Twitter yesterday."

"Christ."

"Yeah. I'd like to bleach my brain, but the good news is his apology was pitch-perfect. Did you guide him through that?"

"Didn't have to. He was pretty emotional all on his own."

"Yes, he would be." She sighed. "He's a good kid. Never gave me any trouble on purpose. But bullshit follows him around like he's cursed. You get that, right?"

"Of course I do."

"What are you going to do about it? The kid needs someone who cares and someone he wants around to help handle him. That gonna be you?"

I cleared my throat. "I hope it is. But he just arrived here yesterday morning, and we spent the time between handling more urgent things. Like the apology."

"Like resolving the unresolved sexual tension between you."

I was silent. It wasn't her business. I knew she'd draw her own conclusions, and she did.

"Well, as you said, he's of age. It's probably for the best. You'll handle him well. You always did. Better than I could, and this is probably why. He wanted to please you. Being around you was more important to him than hanging with idiotic friends or going to parties. If you can be that man for him, God bless you."

"I want to try."

"All right, you've got my blessing, not that you needed it from me. North has a place in my heart. I never knew I had a maternal bone in my body until I guarded that kid. He's just so sweet and dumb."

"He's pure," I said, guilt for ever thinking similar things stinging me.

"Have it your way. I only wanted to check in on him. I take it he's all right?"

"He's humiliated, refuses to leave the room here at the chalet, and doesn't want to ever go home again."

"Maybe he shouldn't."

"Maybe I agree."

"Hmmph, that family. Well, Southerland and Mrs. Ford don't altogether suck, but those parents are caricatures of human beings.

For someone who isn't even an actress, Ms. Astor carries her weight in the faking-it department in that house."

"I can't argue."

"Keep him with you. Get him out of that life."

"I can try, but he's the Astor-Ford heir, along with Southerland, and I don't think they'll keep their talons out of him forever."

She clucked her tongue before saying she had to go. "My new protectee's got me running around Vegas. She is wearing me *out*."

I coughed a laugh. It wasn't professional for Eleesha to say things like that about her client, but I also knew Ruby Montague, the lead singer of the all-girl band, Glue You, was a handful and a half.

"Enjoy," I said, signing off and ending the call.

After my call with Eleesha, I ended up taking the stairs, holding the coffee pot against my chest as I entered the kitchen again. The radio on the windowsill was playing '80s music, and, next to it, Rhonda leaned out the open window, a lit cigarette in her hand.

As I put the coffeepot down on the island in the middle of the room, Rhonda sucked in the "poison," as Suzanne called it, and steadily blew it away on the wind.

"Wish you and Eric would both stop doing that," I said with a sigh. The scent of cinnamon and Christmas spices filled my nose, almost blocking out the smell of the smoke.

"If wishes were changes," Suzanne said, slamming the refrigerator door shut and eyeing her wife.

"How many times have I tried to stop?" Rhonda asked.

"Thirteen," Suzanne and I answered.

"And how many times have I failed?"

"Thirteen."

"Exactly. Besides, I need my alone time with Eric out by the shed during our smoke breaks."

We both rolled our eyes. Turning to me, Suzanne's brows lowered in confusion. "Is there a problem with your coffeepot? Is the machine in your room broken? And I thought you didn't drink coffee?"

"North does," I said. "But this isn't mine. The guy in room nine shoved it in my hands and told me to get rid of it."

Suzanne and Rhonda exchanged amused glances.

Rhonda said, "Ah, that makes sense," before taking another big inhale from her cigarette.

"Does it?"

"Oh, yes," Suzanne says. "It's ridiculous. We'll tell you more later."

"Good thing I'm a patient guy, or I'd be demanding to know more *now*. He also handed off toilet paper to me yesterday. He's an oddball."

"Odd and in love."

"Oh?" I grinned. "Wait, wait…is that Max? Eric's…" I rolled my hand to illustrate more than I had words to express.

"The very one," Suzanne said.

"Where is Eric?" I asked and, noticing the absence of Suzanne's right-hand man Jerome, I added on a question about him as well.

"Jerome's running to town again, and Eric's trying to keep his head together with all this Max stuff driving him wild."

I laughed. I could only imagine how anxious Eric was. He'd really sweated about what had happened with Max last year. He could overthink with the best of them.

Suzanne swung around to glare at Rhonda. "I'm serious now. Put that poison stick out and shut the window. You'll freeze us all to death."

Molly came trotting in from who knew where, but probably one of the rooms with people. She was smiling her happy I've-been-petted-so much-I've-gone-to-doggy-heaven smile, and she trotted to her water bowl, licking messily before laying down on her bed in the back of the room with a huff.

"No greetings for me, huh?" I asked her. She swung her eyes my way, gave me a sweet look, and put her head down.

"Go on," Suzanne said to Rhonda as she ran water over the stamped-out butt and threw it in the trash. "Get Liam set up with the pastries. I assume that's what you're here for since you two missed breakfast."

"Yeah, he likes to sleep late."

"And he's still afraid to face reality?" Rhonda said, crossing to grab a new tray and starting to put together a tasty-looking array of pastries. My stomach rumbled, and Rhonda winked at me.

The song on the radio ended, and the weather was read—one hundred percent chance of snow, starting mild and growing heavier by nightfall.

"Sounds like it'll be a cozy night with all the guests staying in," Suzanne murmured. "I'll make sure to have plenty of hot chocolate and Irish coffee prepared. I guess I'll need to whip some more cream."

"What's Christmas without snow?" Rhonda said, just as the weather report ended and the next song began, raucous and loud.

Suzanne stopped her work on the casserole she was putting together to switch on the twenty-four-hour Christmas music station. It began in November and went through to the New Year. The chime of bells and choral voices fit the aesthetics of the season much better, lending a warm charm to the atmosphere.

"If he's still struggling with anxiety, why not take Molly up with you?" Rhonda said, handing me the tray of pastries, bacon, orange juice, water, coffee, and a hot chocolate for me since I don't like coffee. "She has a way of cheering people up. Always makes me feel better anyway."

Molly lifted her head in interest at the sound of her name and the sight of the food-laden tray. She cocked her head, ears flicking back, and shiny dark eyes lighting up.

"That's a great idea." I kissed Rhonda's cheek and blew Suzanne a kiss. "I'm going to get him to leave the room today, come hell or high water. With any luck, he'll be at the dinner table tonight."

"I sure would love to see his pretty face," Suzanne said, smiling.

"Especially since we saw all his ugly stuff already." Rhonda wrinkled her nose.

"Hey now, I'll have you know what you saw is first class, gorgeous stuff. You're lucky to have seen it."

"What gay men and straight women want with those sticks and berries is beyond me."

Suzanne chuckled. "For that, I'm very grateful."

Rhonda gave her a kiss on the cheek. "Good luck with your man. And bring the tray and plates down when you're done. Eric's a little salty about having to pick them up from outside your door."

I saluted and whistled for Molly. "Come on, girl. I've got a new friend for you."

CHAPTER TWELVE
North

I WOKE UP alone again, and this time there was no note, but I knew Liam had probably gone for food and he'd be right back. Still. While lying in bed, staring at the ceiling, anxieties slipped into my bloodstream, beating with my pulse.

What if the apology hadn't gone as well as Southerland had made it out? What if I could never go on the internet again without seeing my own junk? What if, what if—

They fed into each other on a loop until I got up, slipped on a pair of sweats—the last clean pair I'd thrown into my bag—and a T-shirt, paced around the room three times, and grabbed my phone out of the drawer I'd stuffed it back into yesterday once we'd promised not to look at the internet anymore.

But that was yesterday, and this was today. I needed to know whether I was going to live in this chalet for the rest of my life or if some new scandal had broken which might take the heat away from me.

Twitter was the first app I opened. If anything were going to be trending higher than my dick, it'd show up there first, though TikTok wouldn't be much further behind. I looked at the trending topics, and my hopes rose until I hit the last topic on the list: #NorthsPole

I clicked it. I couldn't help myself.

After a couple of days of avoidance mode, I was confronting the problem head-on. I winced to see that, yes, only a few scrolls down provided me with the photo of my cock. I studied it, trying to understand why it was important to the world at large. I mean, it wasn't like it was my dad's cock. He was the famous actor with girls and guys swooning over him.

But I knew why. It'd been drilled into me since I was a kid.

Because of who my parents were, because I was handsome, because I was rich—people would care.

And, oh boy, did they care. There were threads and threads of discussion about my mishap, my penis shape, the ethics of sharing the picture, of talking about the picture, of not talking about the picture, and to my surprise, there were threads of kindness too. People actually addressing me and saying they hoped I was okay.

A lump grew in my throat.

People wanted me to be okay. Strangers, even.

I opened one such thread reading about how the person was worried for me because I looked devastated in my apology, and they hoped I was all right. Another person said they were praying for me. It felt good to know someone was asking God to heal my heart instead of begging him to punish me.

The key sounded in the door, and I nearly dropped my phone. Busted looking at the internet when I'd promised not to.

But the person who entered wasn't Liam. It wasn't even a person.

A big, floppy golden retriever trotted in, tail wagging and tongue lolling out. Liam was right behind, breakfast tray in hand. I got down on the floor to dig my hands into the dog's fur. "Who's this?"

"That's Molly. She's the chalet's mascot."

"She's so cute!" I petted her and let her get up in my face, sniffing at my hair and neck, making me giggle and squirm. "And friendly!"

"She's a good girl. I thought she might cheer you up.

I looked up at Liam, giving him a smile that seemed to make him feel easier about my state of mind.

"You're feeling better already," he said with a laugh. "I knew she'd do the trick. You always liked dogs. I remember the first time I ever saw you. You were playing with Tyson."

"Tyson was a good boy."

"He was."

"And she's great, too," I cooed, patting Molly some more. "Being with you also helped." I bit my lower lip and snuck a flirty glance from beneath my lashes, hoping to somewhat distract him from what I said next. "And—" I went ahead and copped to it. "I looked online."

"Oh?" He looked as if he was bracing himself. "And it was all right?"

"There was a lot of terrible stuff, but there was some good stuff too. Some people actually seemed to care about whether or not I'm okay. Like, they were genuinely kind about it. I didn't expect that. I thought…" I shrugged. "I don't know. I guess I thought they'd all hate me now, or judge me, or make fun of me forever."

"I'm glad you found some good people in the world. There are still some out there," Liam said, placing the tray on the table and taking a seat. "Like the people here at Camp Bay Chalet. They're good people who would only wish good things for you."

"Maybe the owners, but…" I wrinkled my nose, standing and moving to the seat opposite him, much to the frustration of Molly, who followed and pressed her head on my knee once I was settled. "The guests? I don't know. I can't go out there yet. Not yet."

I patted Molly's head and dug into the breakfast Liam had brought. Whoever provided the pastries to the chalet were magic bakers because each bite tasted like it was dusted with delight. I wondered if my dragons could make room for drawings of magic bakers. For some reason, the idea appealed to me. Happy, cheerful bakers, with flour and scattered glitter dust in the air... I could paint that. It'd be weird and pretty.

"What are you thinking about?"

"Painting magical bakers," I answered.

Liam's lips quirked, but when he looked up, he said, "Would the bakers be dragons?"

"No, people. But dragon bakers are interesting. What kind of pastries do you think they'd like?"

"They'd hoard *all* the pastries."

"Of course." I laughed and gave some of the iced bun I was eating to Molly.

"I won't tell Suzanne about that." Liam laughed. "She's a stickler for Molly not getting treats outside her dinner and breakfast."

"From the look of Molly, I think she gets plenty of treats."

"Oh, for sure. The guests can't resist. And neither can Rhonda."

"Rhonda and Suzanne sound really cool." I picked at the bacon. I liked it, but thinking of how Rhonda and Suzanne were his second family, my mind drifted to his first family, his biological one. "What does your mom think of you being here with me?"

Liam's face twitched. "She's fine with it, of course."

"You didn't tell me the whole truth." I wasn't a genius, but I could always read Liam.

"She wants me home to watch the kids." Liam rolled his eyes. "But that's not my problem. I mean, it's my *job*, in a way, but it's one I do for love. I don't even get paid to deal with those sweet stinkers. I watch them in exchange for room and board." He smiled fondly. "I love them, but they're not truly my responsibility. They're Maeve's kids."

"You don't have a job?" I asked, my gut curling into a knot. "Ever since I fired you?"

Liam reached out to card his fingers through my hair. "I've had jobs. I *have* jobs, even. They're just the kind of work where I set my own hours. Maeve and Mom have seen fit to fill those hours with small monsters for me to keep out of trouble."

"You don't mind?"

"Keeping people out of trouble is part of what I was trained to do. Aiden and Jack are just a bit smaller, is all."

"But—"

"Shh. Enough," he said sternly. "I'm fine. I promise."

"What paid jobs do you have?" I asked.

"I do some rent-a-cop stuff with several local ski resorts, but it's gig work for me, so it's not a constant. Also, in the summer, I do freelance tours of Lake Pend Oreille. It's relaxed and fun. I get to be out on the lake. It's all good."

"It doesn't sound like you make much money."

"Well, that's why I have to earn my food and board." Liam sighed. "Look, after I left working for you, I just didn't want to invest in anyone else like that ever again."

"You think you'd fall—um, extra-care about your next protect-ee, too?" I asked, a flash of insecurity sizzling in my veins.

Liam laughed. "Of course not. I just—" He took a moment. "Look, being with you all the time, seeing the way things are with your family, with the friends you chose, but being unable to do anything about any of it? It was a lot to deal with emotionally. And that's how it would be with whoever else I protected. Honestly, I didn't want to feel that helpless again. It's a part of the job I didn't know about before I'd committed to the work. But now? No. Keeping someone safe in body, but not being able to do anything about their mind or spirit?" He shook his head. "It's too much."

"You don't like being a bodyguard?"

"No, I don't. That's why I haven't gone back to it." Liam touched my cheek, cupping my face. "I don't want to be *your* bodyguard either. I want to be someone who can step in when the going gets rough, help you handle problems, and truly take care of you. I want to be able to tell your mom and dad to back the hell off and—"

"You'd tell them that?"

"Every day if I had to. I want to keep your mind and spirit safe. Even if it's from them."

"They like you," I offered.

"I admit, I'm surprised they don't have opinions about whether or not I'm in this for the money, but—"

"Oh, they've had prenups arranged for Southerland and me for years, and the trusts are set up in a way only certain people can access them, and those people can never be our spouses. You'd be out of luck if you were in it for the money anyway."

"Good. I wouldn't want anyone having doubts I'm in this for you." He chuckled. "So we're getting married, huh?"

"What?"

"You said there are prenups to sign already."

My heart beat hard. "Are you proposing?"

"I thought you were," he teased.

I stared at him, my heart racing, my mind a muddle.

Seeing my confusion, Liam's expression grew more serious. "Baby, my heart has been yours a long time, but it would be premature to do anything permanent quite yet, right?"

"Your heart's mine?"

Liam smiled shyly, and my blood fizzed like champagne in my veins. "I love you. I know it's early, and we haven't seen each other in three years, but you're the same boy I fell for, and my feelings haven't changed. I hope this isn't too—"

"I love you, too." I couldn't keep it back. I reached out to grasp his hands, a lump in my throat. "And you're the same man I fell in love with. You take such good care of me, even now, and—" My voice started shaking, and my eyes pricked with tears.

I rose from the table and pulled Liam up with me. He wrapped his arms around me, and I snuggled close, smelling and kissing the soft skin on his neck. Molly watched us with wide eyes. "I love you," I muttered. "And my heart's yours too. And my body!" I added. "Whenever you want my body, you can have it."

Liam laughed. "I'm afraid we'll never leave this room again if I say the same to you."

"Would that be so bad?"

Liam kissed me, and my knees went weak before he whispered against my lips, "Yes, because I want us to do other things together, too. Everything. Not just naked things."

I nodded, though a foolish part of me felt disappointed, too. I'd love to spend every day of my life naked with Liam. I'd be happy to stay right here in this room, stripped bare and making each other come. What could be better than that look on Liam's face when he'd unloaded into my mouth?

I itched with the urge to see it again.

But I knew what he meant, too. I wanted to do everything with Liam. All the things they showed lovers doing in the movies: going to the beach, buying a house, adopting a pet. I wanted to be in his warm, soothing presence for the rest of my life. Let him take care of me. Let him support me.

In return, I'd give him all the love in my heart, defend him against his mother and sister taking advantage of him, and tell anyone who would listen what a good, wonderful, kind man he is and how he makes my life better just by being in the room.

"What are you thinking? You look worried."

"I'm thinking you're right."

"Yeah?"

"Yeah. There's probably more to life than sex." I rose to my toes and kissed him. "I want to share all of it with you, too. So I guess I have to leave this room eventually."

"'Probably' more to life than sex," Liam whispered with laughter twinkling in his eyes again. "'Probably.'"

"It's so good," I defended. "I didn't know sex could ever be so good. And it's with *you*. I don't want it to be with anyone else. You make me come so hard."

Liam's eyes grew heated, and when he kissed me, I thought we were going to head back to bed for sure. But then Molly let out a little bark, reminding us she was there watching.

We broke apart and sat down again, still holding hands, though, like idiots who couldn't stop touching in case it broke the spell. I wanted to cry. I loved being in love, and having Liam love me back was too good to be true.

Liam finally let go of my hand and went back to eating. He indicated I should eat, too. "When we finish breakfast, how about I sneak us out of here, and we go on a walk? The weather is cold but gorgeous, and there's snow on the way. It's magical on Lake Pend Oreille when it snows."

I squirmed, but Molly propped her big head on my knee again, looking at me imploringly. "Can Molly come?"

"She wouldn't have it any other way."

I bit my lip, imagined myself leaving the room, going downstairs, and being spotted by strangers who'd seen my hard dick. My gut lurched anxiously.

But I couldn't stay in this room forever, even if I wanted to, and Liam would be with me. He'd love me no matter what those people said or thought, and I really did feel cooped up. A walk would be great, and the lake was supposed to be beautiful. I should see it.

"All right."

The smile that cracked over his face was sweet and perfect. Despite my nerves, I was glad I'd said yes, and I allowed him to start dressing me in our less-than-fresh clothes.

Layers were the key, he told me. Lots of layers.

CHAPTER THIRTEEN
Liam

NORTH'S BEHAVIOR AS we left the room would have been comical if it weren't heartbreaking. He had his hoodie pulled up and tightened so you couldn't really see his face—just his eyes and nose and lips. Despite the absurdity of it and me trying to convince him he'd draw more attention looking like that than just confidently walking through a room with his head up, he ignored me and went on trying to hide his face.

We walked down from the third floor with Molly at our heels, and at the top of the flight down to the lobby is where North stalled. Christmas carols and voices—laughter and conversation—drifted up from below. North covered what little could be seen of his face and shook his head. "I don't think I can do it. What if they all know? What if they've seen it?" he whispered.

"Baby, it's going to be okay." I put my arm around his shoulder and pulled him into a hug. Molly snuffled around our legs before sitting down on her haunches to watch us curiously.

North rested there, with his face in the crook of my neck, until I pulled away and said, "Okay, wait here. I'll go down with Molly. I have a plan, okay?"

"What kind of plan?"

"To distract everyone. When the coast is clear, I'll motion for you to come down."

He huffed gently, rubbing Molly's head and gazing into her eyes a moment as if looking for reassurance from her. "Yeah, all right."

"Okay. C'mon, Molly. I need you."

She followed at my heels, looking back twice to see if her new friend North was coming too and seeming worried when he wasn't. The lobby was bustling with a few late-arriving guests for the weekend, and the couches by the fireplace were full of cocktail- and cocoa-drinking lodgers in pajamas, eagerly awaiting the expected storm. I glanced back up at North. He gazed down at me before glancing back over his shoulder in paranoia.

Motioning for him to wait before approaching the check-in desk. I honed in on a certain basket I knew was kept behind the desk and gave Sal a wide smile as he tried to deal with Blustery Bill's running commentary on why the prediction for snow was overblown while also checking Felicity Powers and her daughter Olivia into the chalet.

I grabbed a dingy tennis ball from the basket—one of Molly's toys—without Sal noticing and patted him on the shoulder. He obviously wanted to grill me about what was going on with North, but he didn't have time as Bill continued blabbing.

Back at the bottom of the stairs, I checked North was still there and winced to see another gay couple walking past him and starting down the stairs. North leaned "casually" against the wall, looking strange and out of place with his hoodie over his head and tight around his face. The taller of the two—a devastatingly gorgeous guy who must have been a model—looked back at him a few times, but his husband—judging by the rings on their fingers—tugged him along, murmuring something in his ear.

They passed me at the bottom of the stairs.

"You don't think we should ask at the desk about him?" the blond one asked. "He seems shady."

"I'm sure he's fine, Walker," the probable model murmured. "I think he looks familiar. Maybe he's a celebrity hiding out here."

Walker still appeared doubtful. "There are a number of celebrities of all sorts here. That's what makes it exclusive. Or so my mother said."

"So far, I've just seen the ghost hunter guy from TV." The probable-model looked back over his shoulder. "But he just seems familiar."

"Or criminal."

"Oh!" Model-guy clapped his hands over his mouth. "I know. I recognize him now, and I know just why he has his face covered." He put his hand to whisper in his husband's ear as they reached the last step.

"Ohhh." Walker looked over his shoulder, taking in North peering down from the next floor, his face still mostly hidden, but enough of his features visible that, yes, he was still recognizable. "I see."

"Don't look at him. You'll embarrass him."

Walker rolled his eyes. "Ashton, if anyone's embarrassing him, it's you and all this whispering over him."

They passed by me, and I caught and held North's gaze. He jerked his head for me to come toward him, obviously wanting to retreat to his room again. I shook my head, giving him a gesture meaning, "give me one more minute," and he reluctantly nodded.

I spotted Molly. She'd gone over to the fireplace area, looking adorable, trying to get Teri—a horsebreeder from Montana who came every year—to share her gingerbread cookie. My mouth watered at the sight of it. I loved the chalet's gingerbread cookies. I'd have to grab a few from the kitchen before they were all gone.

I whispered, "Molly, c'mere."

Her ears twitched, and her eyes darted my way for a moment, but she ignored me in favor of the possible cookie crumbs.

I tutted. "You little beggar. C'mere. Come on."

She hefted herself up with a sigh and came to me, her eyes clearly asking if this was going to be worth it for her. I patted her and whispered she was good while watching to see what Sal was doing. He was distracted, taking a credit card from Felicity, so—

I threw the ball toward all the guests resting in the seating area across from the check-in desk. Molly didn't hesitate. She darted after the ball, knocking over Felicity's luggage and nearly tripping Olivia as she took a step back from the check-in desk.

The ball bounced willy-nilly, and Molly dove for it too forcefully, making it bound and fly around the area. The guests gasped, laughed, took cover, and called for her as Sal urgently whistled. The folks gathered around the fireplace stood to get a better look at the chaos, and I motioned North down the stairs in a hurry.

Once he reached me, I tugged him around the corner into the empty events room and rushed him out the back doors and onto the long, wide porch overlooking the lake. We broke out running like we were kids escaping punishment, and we darted toward the lake, both of us laughing. Halfway there, North called for me to slow down so he could untie his head.

Eventually, I did, and he caught up, pushing the hoodie away. I grinned into his beautiful face. If I'd thought the man inside was a possible model, North could be as well. He was just perfect in every way. I adored the cut of his jaw—currently heavy with the new growth since he'd shaved for the apology video—and the sharp, blackness of his hair. The way it made everything about him a contrast of pale and dark.

His eyes, too. They were shining in the light of the mid-morning sun, and I loved to see how they glittered. "Hey," I said, reaching out and pulling him close to me. He glanced over his shoulder as if looking for paparazzi. "There's just us here."

"And all those guests inside."

"They aren't going to take pictures of you," I said as I took off one of my gloves and handed it to him. "We're safe."

"What if they do?" He slipped the single glove on. Now we'd

both have one warm hand at least.

"Then they do."

"And what will the internet say?"

"That a hot redhead is banging you somewhere in Idaho."

North thought about that. "I guess that'd be all right. I mean, it'd be true, at least. I don't mind if they know we're having sex." He jutted his chin out. "I'm proud of it. I want the world to know I'm with you." His eyes narrowed. "Why don't we just do it ourselves?"

"Do what?"

"Tell the world that you're fucking me."

"I can't advise *that*," I said, laughing. "But if you want to admit I exist, and you're with me, I'm all right with it."

His eyebrows did a funny little dance as half a dozen expressions flew around his face. "You wouldn't mind? The whole world knowing you're with the guy who posted his dick on the internet?"

"It's a great dick," I told him again. "Attached to an even better human being, and I'm not ashamed of you, North. I'm proud of you." I took hold of his hand. "But there's no one in the world who should care who we are right now or what we're doing. Let's just walk."

"All right."

Sheltered from the last snow by the big boughs above as we walked, the fresh cool air, the crunch of dead leaves beneath our feet, and the sharp scent of oncoming snow gave the moment a crystalline feeling. It was as if we'd stepped through a looking glass and into a winter fantasy.

The way the light played on the lake was one of my favorite things about the view from Camp Bay Chalet's property. As we stepped down to the path taking us to the shore, we were given two options: choose a boat to row out on or take a shady path deeper into the woods.

"The light is never the same from hour to hour," I commented. "And as the seasons change, you get so many colors. There's the gray of winter—the blue, misty, whiteness of it—and the green of summer, all those verdant shades—"

"Verdant?"

"Verdant is like green, but it's also like life. The concept of living greenness."

"Okay," he said, shooting me an admiring glance for simply knowing a word he didn't. He was too in love with me, and it was too easy to impress him. One day he'd know I wasn't that great really, but for now, it thrilled me to have him look at me like that. He was special to me, and being special to him, too, was like touching a live wire of joy.

"And in autumn..." I stopped walking, taking hold of his hands—one gloved and the other not, same as mine—and kissed the knuckles of his bare hand. "It's painted with the most beautiful colors."

North turned his head, taking in the lake before smiling back at me. "I've never tried to paint something real before. It's always just been things from my mind. But maybe I could paint that for you."

"I'd love for you to try."

"We could come back here in autumn and..." he broke off, his face flushing and his eyes lifting to mine. "I mean, if..."

"I think we're both agreed we're all in, yeah? I mean, we can't move in together next week or anything, but—"

"Why not?"

I laughed again. "Because I have to figure out a way to help Maeve with the childcare issue, and we should probably make sure we really love and like each other first, and—"

"We like each other. You know we do. Even if we've been apart a few years, no one knows me like you do, Liam."

"But maybe you don't know *me* so well. I wasn't entirely myself when you employed me. I tried to be professional. What if you don't like the little things about me?"

"I'll like everything about you," North said fiercely. "Forever."

"That's a big promise."

He shrugged. "I might not be a genius, but I'm smart enough to know what we have is special, *and* I know you'll never leave me because I'm stupid or—"

"You're not stupid." I felt guilty for every time I'd ever thought he was. He was precious in his own right. Smart in heart-shaped ways, if not brain-shaped ways. "Don't insult yourself."

He ignored that. "I'm saying you should move in with me."

"And I'm saying I will when we've had more time together. I'm also saying we can come here next October, and you can try your hand at painting the landscape."

North smiled and stopped walking, taking hold of my hand and nuzzling my neck. "All right. That's good enough for now."

We kissed, and the sky and earth dissolved in the heat between us until voices from up the trail into the forest made us break apart.

"C'mon," I said, taking his hand and heading down toward the lake. "Follow me."

CHAPTER FOURTEEN
North

LIAM ROWED US out onto the lake, the mountains standing tall and imposing on either side of us and the chalet looking quaint and festive behind us. My face was cold in the wind. I put up the hood again to cover my cheeks and ears. The clouds were coming in darker, laden with snow, but Liam assured me we weren't out so far it would be dangerous to stay. "The lake stays fairly calm during snowstorms," he said, "unless it's windy. But don't worry. We won't be out too long."

Without a hat or hoodie, Liam's red hair and gingery freckles seemed to almost glitter in the light, and his nose and ears were bright pink with the cold. My heart thumped just looking at him. He took my breath away.

When he stopped rowing, I ached to crawl over to him and hug him tight, but the wobbling of the boat kept me stuck to my seat. I could swim, obviously, having been raised in California, but I didn't think I wanted to wide up falling into this ice-cold lake wearing all the layers Liam had piled on me. He'd been right, though. I was warm enough. Well, everything except my uncovered hand and my nose. I switched the glove again.

Reaching into my front hoodie pocket, I pulled out my cell phone.

"Hey, I thought we were leaving those inside? Ignoring the world?"

"I was going to, but I thought…" I opened the camera app and took some photos of him. "Well, I thought I might want to capture this so I can remember it forever."

Liam smiled. I took a photo of that, too.

"Can we try for one of both of us?" I asked, moving gingerly, hoping the canoe would hold steady. Liam leaned close to me, and the sides of our heads touched. I took the picture.

Looking at it, I realized it was the first one of the two of us ever taken. We were both rosy from the cold, but our eyes glowed like someone had turned on our souls like Christmas was inside us and shining out. Love. I guessed that's what I was seeing. Love and the high of it.

"Show me," Liam asked.

I turned my screen to him, and he grinned.

"Send it to me."

Pulling up his number from the texts he'd sent me before I arrived, I read them over with a weird sense they had been sent forever ago, and yet it had been just yesterday. I very carefully loaded the pic and made sure he was the only one it was going to, and pressed send.

I stared at the notifs on all my social media accounts. There were so many. What if...what if I gave them a reason for there to be even more? But this time, over something different? Something wonderful.

"What are you thinking about?" Liam asked me. "You look terrified."

"I, uh, have an idea."

Liam's ginger brows lifted. "About...?"

I cleared my throat and waved my phone at him. "What if I...post this?"

"Post the picture of us?"

"Yeah. Everywhere. To everything."

He studied me. "Are you ready for that? People will talk, they'll do articles, they'll dig up the past. They'll find out I was your bodyguard, and they'll make a big deal out of it."

I swallowed hard. "The real question is if you're ready. I face it all the time."

Liam sighed, reached for my phone, and opened my various social media accounts. He glanced through past photos, and he handed the phone back. "I'm all right with it. As I said, I have nothing to hide, and I'm proud of being with you."

"They'll find out who your family is. They'll call. They might even show up."

"At Christmas?"

I nodded.

Liam suggested, "Why don't you start small? Post it just to your circle on Insta."

"Really?"

"Well, who's in your circle?"

"Southerland, a few friends from school before I dropped out—though they're more like acquaintances."

"That seems small enough."

I frowned. Something didn't feel right. "That's not what I wanted, though." I put the phone back in my pocket. "Never mind. It's not the right time. You're not ready for it."

"I'm ready for whatever you want. We can handle anything together."

I shook my head. I didn't want him to find out what a pain in the ass it was going to be with me yet. He might change his mind.

We both grew silent, contemplating things. Me this desire to post about him, to change the conversation, and him... Well, I didn't know what he was thinking about.

So I asked.

"I'm thinking about how I want to show you everything about my hometown now you're here, but I know you don't want to go out in public yet."

"What do you want to show me?"

"Oh, just my favorite bakery, and the coffee shop where I used to go and pretend to smoke cigarettes with my dumb buddies when I was a teenager, and—"

"You smoked?"

"Pretended to." Liam shook his head. "It was ridiculous." He grinned. "I could introduce you to some of those guys. Well, a few of them." A sigh went through him. "Some of them—the majority—peaced out when they found out I was gay. But Silas and Caleb stuck around. They live over in Clark Fork." He laughed. "They're a couple now, so I guess that explains why they didn't run when I came out. The rest? Fuck 'em."

"Fuck them," I murmured. Anyone who cut Liam out of their lives had really missed out.

"But yeah. I'd love to show you the best view of the lake, too. It's—" he pointed, "over that way." Liam paused and licked his lips. "And I want you to meet my mom."

"Your mom?" My heart jolted.

I'd managed to forget that being with Liam meant I'd have to meet the people closest to him. Like his mom. And his twin sister. I didn't know why, but I was sure his sister and mom would hate me.

After what I'd done to Liam, especially. If someone had fired Southerland the way I'd fired Liam—during a pandemic, in this economy!—I'd hate them. Not that Southerland would ever need to work, but it was the principle of the matter.

The kids, though. I could stand to meet the kids. I liked kids. They're cute. "Your mom?" I asked again, my voice breaking.

"And Maeve, and Jack and Aiden. They'll love you."

"No, they won't. I fired you. You're living at home because of me."

"And they ought to be grateful for that. They've wrangled three years of free childcare from me."

"Won't they hate me when they realize I'm going to be the reason they won't have free childcare anymore?"

He laughed. "Oh, baby, don't worry. We'll figure it out. We always do. We Kellys are hardy and resourceful folk."

"I could pay for the childcare."

Liam shook his head, a smile still on his lips. "No way. That's not how this will go down. I won't be a bought man. Just a kept one."

I tilted my head. "Huh?"

"I just mean, I don't need you to give my mom and Maeve a dowry of paid childcare in exchange for my hand in yours."

"Dowry?"

Liam waved it off. "I'll explain all that later. I mean, I don't want you to feel like you have to give money to my family. I won't leave here until something is arranged that's good for everyone."

"If you don't take my money, how will this work out?" I motioned between us.

"I'll get a job."

"You don't need to do that. I want you to take care of me. I want you to be my manager, and that comes with a salary. A good one."

Liam hesitated. "I want to take care of you, too, and I promise I will, but I want to do it for *love*, not money."

"It can be for both."

"This is a weird conversation to be having on a romantic boat ride," he teased. "Let's just agree on one thing for now, and we can hash out the rest later. Will you agree to meet my mom?"

I took in a shaky breath, adrenaline pumping through me. What would his mother be like? Would she look like Liam? I wanted to meet her so I could understand him even better, and I dreaded it because I knew in my heart she wouldn't approve.

Because she'd seen my dick.

Everyone had.

That was a hurdle bigger than any upset about jobs or money or childcare. My dick was emblazoned in her mind, and I didn't think I could look her in the eye.

But when I opened my mouth, prepared to explain why I had to say no, I was silenced by the hope in Liam's eye. It would mean a lot to him. It was written all over his face. He really wanted me to meet his mom.

"All right."

"Good," he said as he let out a sigh. "Because I'd already promised her I'd bring you home for Christmas."

"What?" I squawked. "I said I'd meet her; I didn't—"

Liam leaned forward carefully, the boat still swinging back and forth in a way that made my belly swoop. "Hey, I'm going to be with you. It's all right. She's dying to meet you. She's going to love you, I promise."

"And Maeve?"

"She's going to be a tougher nut to crack," he admitted, his lips hovering close to mine. "But you'll make her crumble in the end. I just know it."

The kiss was soft, sweet, and made me want to melt into a puddle at the bottom of the canoe.

"Hey, give me your phone," Liam said, his breath puffing against my lips.

I reached into my pocket and handed it over to him. With the fingers on his bare hand, he opened it again, showed me the hookup app that'd been the cause of my humiliation, and, as I nodded, he deleted it from my phone.

He opened Insta, created a new post, uploaded the photo of us, and handed the phone back to me with the cursor blinking. "Go on," he encouraged. "I'm ready if you are."

With trembling fingers—from cold and excitement—I typed in: *Spending Christmas Eve's Eve in a canoe with my boyfriend.*

I posted it to my close circle and slipped my phone back into my pocket.

As we kissed again, tongues and lips hot in the cold air, vibrations went off in my pocket. But this time, they didn't feel threatening.

They felt like celebratory fireworks.

EVENTUALLY, WE WERE too cold and the boat too wobbly, so Liam set off back for the chalet, his arms moving powerfully, shoving the water aside and propelling the canoe onward.

As we came to shore, it started to snow.

Rushing back up toward the porch, not to avoid the snow but to claim the rocking chairs there and watch it start to really come down, I felt dizzy with excitement. Liam, for his part, also seemed happy, glowing like a kid showing off his favorite present from Santa. He sat in the rocking chair next to me, both of us panting from the run up the hill, laughing.

"This is amazing," he said. "In one way, I can't get used to you being here with me, but in another, it feels like I never left your side."

As my phone continued to buzz with notifications, I hoped he wouldn't regret our choice to go public. "You're honestly not embarrassed by me?"

"Baby…" Liam rolled his eyes slightly and shook his head. "Never."

"What if I'd posted my asshole instead?"

"I mean, it's a gorgeous asshole," he shrugged, "but I'd like to keep it just between us if you don't mind."

I smiled.

Holy shit, at least I hadn't posted my asshole. Although, was that really worse than my dick?

The back door opened, and the owner, Rhonda, came out with two mugs with candy canes sticking out of them and a big grin. "Hot cocoa," she explained, handing them over to us and looking at Liam expectantly.

"North, this is Rhonda. My former boss and other mother."

She seemed pleased, but she slapped his shoulder and rolled her eyes like she was obligated to in case she came across as cheesy.

"It's nice to meet you," I said, offering my hand and shaking firmly.

She's seen my dick, she's seen my dick, she's seen my dick.

Heat pricked my cheeks, and my lips trembled as the humiliation hit me. But Rhonda didn't seem to notice. She just smiled at me and said, "I hope you know by now how welcome you are here. We would love it if you could make it to lunch or dinner tonight. Our guests are all open-minded and kind people." She hesitated. "Well, for the most part. But you're a welcome addition." She patted my hand, winked at Liam, and went back inside.

"She's seen my *dick*."

"She's a lesbian. She'll have no opinion on it other than 'not my cuppa.' But, baby, more than that, she is a genuinely kind woman, and I know her heart goes out to you. Please consider the idea that not everyone's going to hold this against you. Remember what you saw online earlier. There are people who do care about how this affects you and just want you to feel better."

I nodded, but my throat was tight, and I couldn't seem to swallow down the lump. The tears in my eyes were embarrassing, too. Not because I was in front of Liam but because the couple who'd passed me on the stairway earlier came outside. The dark-haired, gorgeous one greeted us with an exclamation about the snow and questions about the likelihood of a white Christmas.

"We're really getting lucky this trip, aren't we, Walker?" He turned to me and put out his hand. "Hi, y'all. I'm Ashton Sellars."

"Liam Kelly."

"Walker Ronson."

Handshakes went around before it was my turn to speak up. "Hi, I'm, uh, North Astor-Ford." Panicking, I blurted, "And, yes, that's my dick you've seen."

Liam went still next to me, and Ashton's stunning eyes flew wide. Walker coughed and looked away at first, but after a beat, he put his arm around Ashton's shoulders and met my gaze again, his expression kind and empathetic.

"You're so honest," Aston said, patting my shoulder and grinning. He was a little flamboyant in his movements, and he spoke with a mild lisp. "I love that for you." He squeezed my arm. "Do you mind?" He indicated the empty rockers.

I shook my head. He took the rocker on the other side of me. His boyfriend, Walker—no, husband; the matching rings said they were married—took the other open rocker next to him.

Ashton said, "Since you brought up the elephant on the porch, so to speak, I just want you to know you made a very good apology. When we saw you lingering on the stairs earlier, I recognized you, and I admit I took a look-see on my phone about the latest news about you and obviously was greeted with a helluva lot of opinions regarding your—ahem, incident. But after your apology video, you seem exonerated of any wrongdoing by many, if not all, of the randos online."

"Thank you?" I didn't know what to say, though I was relieved to hear it. It was all so embarrassing.

Thankfully Ashton changed the topic. "Anyway, Walker and I are here for our anniversary." He sent his husband a glowing look of love. "Three years officially together on Christmas Day. We got *married* on Christmas Day, too. It's a thing for us."

"Nice," Liam said, by way of encouraging conversation, I guessed.

Ashton took Walker's hand and kissed the back of it, and Walker winked at him with a sweetness that made my own tummy flip.

Being in the presence of people in love made me feel my own new love even more. My jittery joy awakened again, and I couldn't help but look toward Liam to find he was looking at me, too.

"Walker's parents gave us this trip as a first-anniversary gift. So far, it hasn't been a letdown." Ashton smiled, and I was blinded by it. He had an unforgettable face, unlike his husband, who was, to be fair, just kind of average-looking.

"Three years together," Liam said. "How did you meet?"

"We were business partners," Walker said in an even tone.

"An office romance!" Ashton exclaimed, elevating the story immediately with his enthusiasm. "We were a rom-com cliché in every way."

"How about you two?" Walker asked. "Is this new?"

"Yes, you're both glowing." Ashton grinned.

Liam cleared his throat and seemed about to dodge the question. I didn't know why, but I didn't want him to deny our beginning, even if it was probably "wrong" in the eyes of society. I blurted out, "He was my bodyguard in high school. I fell in love with him then."

Their eyebrows did interesting things, and I knew what they were imagining.

"But it wasn't like that," I rushed to explain.

"We were just employer and employee," Liam elaborated. "But eventually, yes, our feelings changed from professional to less than professional, so I left service with him."

"For three years, he's had nothing to do with me. Wouldn't even answer my texts." I pouted.

"And now…" Liam smiled, turning happy eyes my way. "Now the time is right."

"You mean his age is right?" Ashton asked, and it somehow sounded more like a brutal tease than an accusation in his light voice.

"*Everything's* right," Liam corrected. "Some things just take time. This between us—" he took up my hand and kissed the back of it as Ashton had done to Walker, "—was worth waiting for."

My heart melted, and I gave him a sloppy grin.

The door opened with a mild squeak, and Rhonda stepped back out to the porch, this time with candy-cane-garnished mugs for Ashton and Walker. Molly was at her heels, and we all petted her. Ashton and Walker chatted with Rhonda asking questions about Molly—her age, her breed, how she and Suzanne had chosen her.

They broke out their phones and started showing her pictures of their own dogs. One poodle, two beagle mixes, and a golden doodle. A *lot* of dogs. Liam and I looked at them, too, and agreed they were all very cute. We both had to confess to being currently petless.

"No dogs, but I have nephews," Liam offered as Rhonda excused herself to go help in the kitchen. He opened photos of Jack and Aiden. I realized it was the first time I'd seen them. "They're just as rambunctious as puppies, from what I understand. Just as messy, too."

My heart did funny things when Liam showed a photo of him holding the baby with the other boy using him like a climbing tree. The one he identified as Aiden hung from his extended arm, and Liam grinned joyfully. All three were so cute, and one of the boys looked like he could've been Liam's own son; there was such a resemblance.

Suddenly, I was eager to meet them on Christmas Day when Liam took me home with him. Even if I did have to endure the humiliation of being seen by Liam's mom and sister, knowing they not only had opinions about me for letting Liam go the way I had but knowing they'd seen my hard dick, too. I shrugged the thought away and went back to listening to Liam and our couple of acquaintances talk about dogs.

As the snow started to paint the yard white, Liam and I stood to go in, and Ashton held my hand longer than necessary. He peered into my eyes, saying, "I've had a lot of experience with humiliation myself, and I'm going to share a little advice that you can take or leave. I just know it's helped me."

"All right."

"Just surrender to it. Stop resisting. It's done. It's over. Pretend like every single person you meet for the rest of your life has seen it, and just *own* that. You'll be shocked how strong it feels to *just not care anymore.*"

I was somewhat annoyed by his unwanted advice, but I thanked him anyway.

Despite wanting to dismiss his words and go right back to being panicked and paranoid, when I *did* walk back inside with Liam next to me, I heard Ashton's voice in my mind. *Just own that.*

Yes, multiple heads turned my way, including the guy at the check-in desk who'd asked for my father's signature. I lifted my head and looked every person in the eye. *They've seen my dick. All of them.* I took another breath. *So what?*

I wasn't sure I believed myself, but it was enough for now.

I followed Liam upstairs to our room, where he took me in his arms as soon as the door was shut behind us. Ten minutes later, I was lost in a haze of pleasure. Full of gratitude that one man, in particular, was now *very* familiar with my dick.

CHAPTER FIFTEEN
Liam

A FTER NORTH AND I had warmed our cold bodies up back in the room, we'd taken a short nap before heading down to lunch together.

The dining room was set up as it always had been, with four tables that could accommodate ten but were currently set for eight. It warmed my heart to think Rhonda had set places for North and me in hopes he'd be willing to come out of his hidey-hole again. I was sure she'd set places for him at every meal since he'd checked in and for me since I'd arrived.

We took the open seats next to Ashton and Walker at table three since North seemed comfortable with them now, and as we took our seats, we were introduced to Pierce Hunter and Haven Sage. They were another queer couple, this time from Pennsylvania. North's shoulders visibly relaxed as it became clear neither of them recognized him at all. Though, I recognized Pierce. He was the star of my favorite ghost-hunting show.

While we waited for Rhonda, Jerome, Suzanne, and Sal to bring lunch around to place in the middle of the tables family style, Ashton, Walker, and I chatted lightly with our new acquaintances.

"What's your verdict?" Walker asked Pierce after his boyfriend, Haven, mentioned they were looking into rumors of a ghost at the inn. "As a professional ghost hunter, do you think Camp Bay Chalet is haunted?"

"I'm not ready to make that call quite yet," Pierce said. "We'll have to run more tests first."

Haven interrupted him, laughing. "In other words, you'll have to watch the next season of *Paranormal Hunters* to find out what he really thinks."

A shiver ran through North, and I squeezed his thigh again beneath the table.

"It's a pretty tame story overall," Pierce replied. "The man who built the chalet back in the thirties, Joseph Morton, put all four of his sons to work on it with him. It took eight long years to complete it, facing setback after setback. And when it was done, Joseph only got to sleep in the finished chalet for two nights before he died of what appeared to be a heart attack."

"Was it murder?" North asked quietly.

"No, it was a heart attack," Pierce said. "But rumor has it, he haunts the house to this day. Now, in the middle of the night..." Pierce's voice lowered, adding a hint of spooky drama to his words. "In Room Eight, and *only* Room Eight, you can hear his *hammering.*"

North took hold of my hand and squeezed it.

A high-pitched laugh fell from Ashton's mouth. He looked unnerved as well. "Now that I'm going to be up all night listening for ghostly hammering let's move on from scary talk. Haven, what is it you do?"

"Oh, you'll have no luck there," Pierce said with a twinkle. "Go on, tell them."

"I'm a horror writer." Haven's eyes were pleasantly humorous.

North was predictably quiet while we continued to wait as the rest of the guests filed into the dining room.

The food had just been placed at our table, much to everyone's relief since we were all growing hungry, when an older couple came in apologizing for being late. I recognized them as Mr. and Mrs. Tottenham, semi-regulars for Christmas at Camp Bay Chalet, and noted celebrity hunters.

If Pierce could find a ghost anywhere in the world, Mrs. Tottenham could find a celebrity. As she took a seat at our table, she did a double take, complete with a narrowing of her eyes as she took in both Ashton and North speculatively.

"Which one is famous?" She whispered overloudly to her husband.

Mr. Tottenham pondered them both, making North squirm. "The tall one."

North was plenty tall but not as tall as Ashton. Mrs. Tottenham's attention fell on Ashton entirely, and Ashton rolled with it. He winked and waved to her with just his fingers.

Walker whispered in his ear, and Ashton pretended to be bashful, pushing against his husband and almost blushing. "You're so sweet! Any sweeter, and you're going to make me gain weight, and I can't afford it! You know the camera adds ten pounds!"

"Camera?" Mrs. Tottenham asked. "Are you on television?"

"Movies," Ashton said, his eyes twinkling.

"Oh? Anything I've seen you in?"

Walker gripped Ashton's arm, but there was an undeniable smirk on his face as if he knew there was no stopping his man from saying whatever he was going to say next.

"Are you familiar with Honeypot Productions?"

Mrs. Tottenham shook her head.

"Ah, they're an up-and-coming gay porn outfit, and I'm their number one star."

North stiffened and looked at me, his brows high, as he leaned close and said, "I thought he was in advertising."

I shrugged. *I don't know*, I mouthed.

Mrs. Tottenham and Mr. Tottenham froze in place. "I'm sorry? I believe I misheard you," Mr. Tottenham said, cupping his ear.

"No, you heard him just fine," Mrs. Tottenham said, rising

from her seat and spotting two empty chairs at table one. "Come on. There are seats over there, and I'd like to talk to Rhonda about how this establishment has gone downhill. A porn star is not a celebrity," she said sternly to Ashton, shooting us all with dagger eyes.

The old couple gone, Ashton grinned and said to Walker, "Ah, that was fun! Brings back such good memories of our first Christmas together!"

"Lying to people about who we are?" Walker asked with a fondness that removed any sting to his words.

"Misleading them. For the greater good," Ashton said, smiling at North. "We were work partners, but we also had to pretend to be boyfriends for his sister's wedding."

"He's not a porn star, by the way—"

"Not that there's anything wrong with being one," Ashton clarified. "Sex positivity and all the good stuff."

"We're both ad executives. He's just…" Walker smiled, clearly bewildered by his handsome partner even a year into marriage. "Like this."

"And I love that for you." Ashton said to him sweetly before adding, "And for me."

Ashton proceeded to regale Pierce and Haven with the story of how he and Walker had gotten together, and we all dished the food around, eating, laughing, and having a good time.

I could tell lunch had turned out to be easier and more fun than North had thought it would be. Mid-meal we played a game of pin-the-tail on Rudolph, with Rhonda blindfolding the participating guests one by one and sending them toward a big Rudolph poster on the wall with a magnetic tail to stick on. Scott Lennox, a retired pro golfer, if I recalled correctly, won.

Fancy Christmas cocktails were served after the meal was over, and we followed Ashton and Walker out to the common area around the fire for more talking while we finished our drinks.

It was a relief to see North feeling comfortable with anyone at all. I was grateful to these men for bringing him out of his shell.

Later, back in our room, North stood by the window, watching the snow come down. He was fascinated by it. Even though he occasionally saw snow in his new home of Seattle, he'd grown up in California, and the abundance of white wonder Idaho could provide was new to him.

I flipped on the gas fireplace, blue-orange flames leaping up immediately. The chalet could be drafty, and while we'd been perfectly content the first two nights, I knew with the snow coming down and temperatures dropping, we could use some extra warmth. I turned the lights off, letting the glow from the fire light the room.

North kept his back to me, his eyes on the snow, as I peeled off my clothes, folded them on the chair, and laid down on the bed, already hard and wanting him again.

"What if your mom hates me?" he whispered.

"She won't."

North didn't turn around, and I started to stroke myself slowly, wanting to give him a good show when he finally did.

"What if your sister does?"

That was harder to lie about because Maeve did have a grudge against North. In fact, earlier, before dinner, she'd sent a text to me with a clown face emoji and the words *Don't do this to yourself.* I guessed either Mom had told her, or she'd figured out my feelings for North on her own.

"She doesn't know you yet."

North sighed and turned, his eyes going wide. "You're already—" He scrambled at his own clothes—or, rather, my clothes he'd borrowed (and wow, did I love seeing him in my things). He made a mess of undressing, getting caught up in the arms of the white and black Fair Isle sweater he wore.

When he was naked, panting from the effort, his big cock rose up out of his nest of black pubic hair. He was gorgeous—well-built and strong. I took a moment to admire him, working my cock before reaching down to cup my balls. "What do you want to do?"

"I want..." He glanced away shyly.

"Come on, baby. I want to hear what you want."

"I—I want you to handle me."

Reaching out, I pulled him to me. "I'll handle you, all right."

Skin against skin, my mouth pressed against his, and he surrendered to my intensity. As I brought him down on top of me, he whimpered. I stroked my cock alongside his, licking into his mouth and making him moan with need. He was eager, and I was too horny for him. I knew we'd fail to make it last again unless I took control.

So I did.

"Get the lube," I muttered.

"Where?"

I pointed.

North scrambled for the lube on the bedside table where I'd put it the other day and uncapped it. When he was back on his knees, straddling me, he hesitated, looking at me for instruction.

"Put it on your asshole and a little inside it, too."

Shaking, North squirted a ton into his hand, more than enough for most guys but probably not quite enough for a virgin, and obeyed my order. He remained above me, knees planted on either side of my thighs as he worked himself open.

Planting my hand on his thigh, I steadied him. "Have you had anything up there before?"

He blushed, and I was charmed all over again. How could he be so sweet still, after all we'd already done? "Yes."

"You liked it?"

"Oh, yes."

Carefully, I coated the finger of my right hand with lube while he watched, then I gripped his thigh again and moved my slicked-up hand between his legs. Gazing at him, I whispered, "It might feel strange at first."

But if it did, North liked the strangeness. His lower lip rolled between his teeth, and his hard cock flexed, dripping a sweet pearl of pre-cum onto my pubes. "Liam," he groaned as I pressed inside. "Oh, fuck. That's…you're in me."

"I'm going to be even farther in you soon," I whispered.

It didn't take long for North to be sweating, cursing, and clenching around my fingers as I stroked over his prostate and worked him open. He kept grabbing and releasing his cock, as if it was all too much to stroke himself and be fingered at the same time. Still, he continued to leak pre-cum until a small puddle of it wet my pubes and slipped down the inside of my thigh.

When his thighs started shaking, I knew it was time. I needed to get inside him.

He hissed with dismay as I withdrew from his body and then started to make a sweet whining noise when he saw me slicking up my cock with lube. "Liam," he whispered. "Oh, God. Are you going to fuck me?" His voice shook with lust and some nerves.

"I'm going to fuck you," I murmured. "I'm going to be inside you."

He moaned again.

"I'll paint your insides with my cum. And then I'll leave it there. For you."

My words almost ruined the whole thing because North's eyes rolled back. His hips shook, and his cock flexed hard. His balls drew up tight, and I knew he was about to come. I grabbed his balls, squeezing lightly and pulling them down. He broke into a sweat as I managed to stall his orgasm.

"Liam," he whined. "Please. Do it. Do that to me. I don't want to wait anymore."

"Me either." I was flushed all over and sweating with the desire to bury my aching cock in his gorgeous body. "How do you want to take me?"

He didn't hesitate. "On my back."

With trembling limbs, we repositioned ourselves, and when I rose over him, holding my lubed cock in my hand, it was difficult to tear my gaze away from his flushed cheeks and dark eyes to make sure I was lined up properly.

"This is it," I growled. "I'm going to fuck you now, baby. What we've always wanted. What you need."

"Yesssss." He reached for me, and I pushed against his rim.

It was unsuccessful, and North's neck flushed even darker pink from pain or embarrassment; I wasn't sure. "Do it again," he demanded after a second, biting into his lower lip to steel himself.

"It's going to hurt some," I said, patting his hip and encouraging him to relax. "But it gets better."

"I know. I have dildos."

I muffled another laugh. He was so adorable and funny. I loved him. "What do you do to get a dildo in more easily?"

"Breathe out."

"Yeah. Let's try that."

He took a deep breath, gaze on mine, and I leaned forward to press a kiss to his lips, saying, "Now, out."

He let out a long breath, and I thrust forward—slow but hard. The push inside was always good for me, one of my favorite things about a fuck, but with North, it was exquisite. Tears burned. He was so tight, and inside he was hot as blood. I pushed again, moaning as I sunk deep inside. Love hit me like a punch. I threw my head back at the intensity of it. This was me with North. This was me making him mine in every way. I wanted to cry. My heart ached with fullness and joy.

"Fuck," North whispered, eyes rolling back and throat convulsing. "Fuuuuck."

"Mm." I kissed his mouth, but he turned his head away, gulping air. "You okay? It takes a little—"

"It's too good," he said, his voice thick with tears. "You're really here. Inside me. This is you." He squeezed his asshole, and I groaned. "I'm sorry." He wiped a hand over his lashes. "I'm crying. That's dumb, isn't it? I'm dumb."

"No, baby, as long as you're not crying from pain, then it's just..." I kissed his neck, his collarbones, and moved my hips. Light thrusts in and out had him groaning and shaking beneath me. "Then it's just love."

"Love," he moaned. "I love you."

"Oh, North." Tears filled my eyes too. "I've wanted to take care of you like this for so long."

I moved in and out of him gently, only keeping myself from going off like Christmas fireworks by closing my eyes and saying old prayers I'd learned as a Catholic kid terrified of being gay. Now they served to keep me steady.

North shook all over, spasming and clenching beneath me, but his orgasm didn't come quickly at all. In fact, his cock softened at first, and it was only with the work of his hand between us he hardened again. Once it was, he teased himself, keeping on edge, not wanting it to be over.

We fucked slowly, the fire glowing over our skin and the room growing so heated sweat poured from us. We kissed and whispered words of love, tenderness, and promises I hoped we would keep. Letting go of his cock, North clung to me, trembling with ecstasy and letting me rake against his prostate with each thrust until he kicked my ass with his heels and dug his nails into my back. He shook all over, and I kissed his neck, his cheeks, and his lips, watching him come unglued.

"Sweet, beautiful baby," I encouraged him. "That's it. Come apart on my cock. You're so good at this."

The praise seemed to kick him to an even higher ecstasy, and he gripped me, holding me deep, panting and clawing as I whispered in his ear about how hot he felt inside, how I could feel his pulse throbbing on my dick, and how we were joined together now.

"I love you," he sobbed as I began to nail his prostate again. "This is so good. How do you make me feel so good?"

"Love," I told him again. "This is all love."

I was consistent with my thrusts, but it wasn't enough for him.

"I need you inside me," he cried, grabbing his cock again. "Don't go yet. Don't *go*."

"We haven't even come," I reminded him. "We're not even close."

He shook his head. "I'm so close. So, *so* close, Liam."

"Shh," I soothed, removing his hand from his dick. "Stay here with me. Eyes on my face."

The shock of our connected gaze was electric. It burned through my whole body, jolting my cock with pleasure and making my toes curl. We stared at each other as we moved together. In the low light of the room, his irises glowed around the wide darkness of his dilated pupils. I felt as if I could drown in them, as if I was fucking his soul, and he was revealing it all to me through his gaze.

The pleasure between us grew and grew, and finally when North started crying again, pleading, "Please, Liam, I need more. I can't take it. It's so good, please," I increased the tempo.

Faster, faster, pushing into him and pulling out until I was fucking him harder than I thought I probably should. And yet North keened like a man on the edge, and I was so close to orgasm I could feel the buzz of it at the base of my spine, in my asshole, and clenching in my balls.

"Touch yourself," I told him. "Make yourself come."

He didn't hesitate, and when he jerked himself hard and fast, I kissed him. With our tongues and breath intertwined, and our bodies united, the pleasure pooled, spun, grew, and—

"Fuck!" I cried. "Oh, baby, oh fuck!"

North's cum unloaded between our bodies, and he scrabbled at my back with his free hand as he convulsed. His groan was low and loud, guttural as if pleasure was pulled like a knotted string from his dick.

"That's it," I encouraged as he quaked under me. "Give me all you've got."

"Liam," he whimpered.

"I've got you. I've got you, and you're safe with me."

North sighed and held me tight, his hands clenching around my back, smearing the cum from his fingers there.

I pulled out of the kiss, lifting on my elbows to see his face. His eyes were closed, and his mouth hung open, sheer ecstasy all over his features. I moved my hips, feeling the slickness where I'd left my cum inside him. It shouldn't be so hot—but I'd never done that with anyone before. In a way, North took the last of my virginity, just as I took the first of his.

"When I pull out, there'll be some cum that comes out," I warned him.

He lifted his legs and wrapped them around my hips. "No. Stay in me."

"My dick won't stay hard. I'll have to pull out eventually."

"All right," he whispered. "But stay until you can't anymore."

So I did.

My dick made a liar of me. I softened only a little before, feeling North squeeze around me, I got hard again. North did too, and we started the slow grind again, our bodies moving together as pleasure built between us.

We fucked for what seemed like hours and eternities, neither of us growing weary of the slide of our bodies, the heat of our lovemaking. We kissed, and licked, and made quiet pledges to each other.

The second climax was sweeter, softer, and North convinced me to stay in him until I slipped out. But he wasn't ready for it to be over. He stayed next to me, licking my nipples, kissing my neck, and when I finally got hard again, he got on top of me and rode me to his third orgasm of the night. I couldn't get there, the bliss eluding me, but it was gorgeous watching him writhe and jerk himself until his jizz painted my body.

After a long rest, drowsing in each other's arms, North woke me again, curled on his side as the little spoon, and whispered, "Let's skip dinner."

"You'll be hungry later."

"I don't care. Will you fuck me again? I don't think I can come again, but I just really want it."

I'd never been able to deny him anything.

Renewing the lube, we fucked sleepily until we drifted off, another orgasm evading us both, but we stayed connected until I softened. I cuddled him close, sniffing his hair and kissing his shoulder. I loved him so much.

When I woke in the night, stomach growling, wondering if I could get away with sneaking into the kitchen and making a tray for us both, I thought about how unfair it was we ever had to be apart again. I wasn't looking forward to when this weekend was over. But no matter what happened between us, we both had some things to deal with before this could become our life.

Crawling from our bed, slipping on clothes, and heading out the door on my tip-toes, I took the stairs down to the lobby. As I passed the landing for the second floor, I heard some whispering followed by a small cry. I stopped, turning to the darkened hallway, lit by runners along the floor for emergency purposes.

Ashton stood with his hand over his mouth and Walker's arm around him. "Oh my God, I thought you were the ghost!" he whispered loudly, his voice shaking.

"No, just headed down the kitchen."

Ashton let out a whooshing sigh of relief and sagged against his husband. "I'm sorry for shrieking like that."

"No problem." I was curious, though. "What are you doing up and about?"

Ashton looked to Walker, who looked back at Ashton with a very "you tell him" expression.

"Well, we were in the library," Ashton offered.

"Dancing," Walker went on.

"Dancing in the library?"

Ashton waved his cell phone. "Yes, to a Sufjan Stevens' Christmas album—*Silver and Gold*. Do you know it?"

"No?"

"It's good," Walker said.

"Yeah, um, that's what we were doing," Ashton summed up.

I laughed and waved them on. "Well, good night. Sorry I startled you." I had no doubt they'd done a bit more than dancing in the library, but I didn't blame them. It was their anniversary, and they were still so in love. They'd probably begun making out in there and lost track of time.

I could relate. I lost track of time whenever I touched North.

Putting together a small tray of cheese and fruit from the kitchen, I thought about how sex with North felt entirely different from the other men I'd been with. It meant so much more. Every other guy had been focused on getting off with or without me, but North was focused on what it meant for me to be touching him, to be inside him. It was beautiful.

Carrying the tray back up to our room, I thought about how being the first man to make love to North was a thrill, but I knew we were much more than just what our bodies did in bed.

He brought out the best in me, the most generous part of my-self. And I brought out the strength in him. We were good together. Helping North to live a happy life would be a prize beyond measure.

Christmas's greatest gift to me.

CHAPTER SIXTEEN
North

December 24

I HISSED AS I pushed myself out of bed, surprised at the slight twinge of pain from my asshole. It felt as if the muscle of my anus might be slightly bruised.

"Hurting? We fucked a lot last night." Liam asked, reaching for me, concern lowering his brows. He turned me around, questing down between my ass cheeks to touch me there. "Not puffy. Does it sting or—" He motioned at the mattress. "Just bend over the bed and let me have a look."

"No, it's okay," I said, feeling suddenly shy at the idea of bending over and letting him take a gander at my hole. It wasn't as if he hadn't had complete ownership of it just a few hours ago. But it was different in the heat of the moment.

Now, in the coolness of satisfied love and lust, and the clarity of a few hours of sleep, it felt embarrassing. "Everything's fine. Let's just get breakfast—well, lunch now, I guess. We can sit with Ashton and Walker and go for a long walk in the snow. I want to build a snowman or—I know! Let's have a snowball fight! You know I'd win."

"Never. I'd beat you soundly." But Liam looked at the time and groaned. "I'd love to do all that, baby, but we don't have time. We have to be at my Mom's house. We've gotta shower, shave, dress, and drive to Sandpoint."

My stomach tightened. "I thought we were going over tomorrow? Didn't your mom say she wanted me to come for Christmas?"

Liam wiped a hand over his face, worry descending. "I'm sorry. I should have been clearer. My family has celebrated with dinner and presents on Christmas Eve ever since my dad died."

Kneeling by him, I took hold of his hands. I knew Liam's father had died before I met him, but despite him telling me all about his Camp Bay Chalet family when working for me, he'd never opened up much about his biological family.

"When did he die?"

"My senior year of high school."

"I'm sorry."

Liam sighed. "It sucked. We weren't close, but we weren't estranged either. He wasn't happy I was gay, but he was working on accepting it. I think, deep down, he'd always known, though."

I sat beside him, saying nothing because I didn't know what to say. My father was entitled and obsessed with his fame, but he'd accepted me being bisexual easily. I half-suspected he was, too. Well, Southerland did. She was the one who'd told me, and after she'd pointed it out, I agreed.

Also, I couldn't imagine my dad being dead. He was bigger than life. A literal movie star.

"My mom struggled after his death. The first year, we tried to do Christmas like always, but Mom and Maeve cried the whole time. So we decided to create new traditions."

I kissed the back of his knuckles like he kept doing to me.

"That's when we started doing the family presents and dinner on Christmas Eve, and on Christmas Day, we come over here to the chalet. The Christmas Day festivities are open to friends and family of the employees and the guests. Even though I don't technically work here anymore, Rhonda and Suzanne still include my family and me."

I smiled. "Rhonda does seem like a nice person."

"Suzanne is, too. I know you'll like her when you finally talk with her. And Eric, the maintenance man and groundskeeper, is a good pal. And Jerome and Sal. The whole staff. They all take care to make sure my mom and sister feel like they're always welcome here, even when I was working with you in California."

"Wow, that's really nice."

"Yeah. Anyway, now we have our main family celebration on Christmas Eve at my mom's house. I should have let you know. It's different."

"No more different than my family. I mean, my parents 'celebrate' for two weeks straight, so..."

"I remember."

Liam rose and pulled me to standing, running a hot gaze up and down my body. "You're filthy, baby. You need to shower."

I glanced down. My stomach and chest were covered with dried cum. My chest hair, especially, was matted with it. "Yeah. Wow." I chewed on my bottom lip, remembering last night. I was definitely not a virgin anymore. I'd been skewered on Liam's cock over and over, and I'd fallen asleep gripping it in my ass just to revel in the feel of him there.

But now...

I flushed all over, remembering how I'd begged, cried, and made ungodly noises when I'd come. What did Liam think of me now? And what had the neighboring rooms heard? They'd already seen my dick, and now they might have heard my orgasm noises and my horny desperate pleas for Liam to fuck me harder.

"What's wrong? If you don't want to go to my mom's, I can tell her I'm sorry, but neither of us can make it. I'm not leaving you alone here."

"No," I whispered. "I'll go with you."

What had I been thinking to lose control like that? To forget there were people around us? To lose myself in—

"North," Liam said in a slightly sharp, no-nonsense voice. "Talk to me. Did I hurt you? Are you in pain? Let me look."

"No, it's okay," I said. "Last night, I was so loud. Plus, I cried."

"Feelings aren't bad things. You know that. Being overwhelmed and emotional when being intimate with someone you love? That's not a bad thing, either. It takes a lot of courage to be open enough with someone to show them your true feelings."

"It does?"

"Of course."

"Why didn't *you* cry?"

Liam smiled, holding me closer. "I almost did when you were riding me. You looked gorgeous. My baby working himself to orgasm on my cock. Fucking glorious. Best Christmas present of my life."

Heat rushed up my throat and into my cheeks, and I wondered why I was always blushing when *he* was the redhead. "I love you, and it felt so good," I confessed.

"I love you too."

"What if the neighbors heard?"

"They were too busy listening to ghostly hammering or doing their own hammering, I promise."

"But what if they did?"

"This is a romantic chalet. People are going to have sex. But you weren't that loud. These walls are thick—wood logs! I haven't heard a peep from the other guests, and I don't think you have either."

I shook my head. He was right; I hadn't.

"Don't worry about it."

"Okay." I hesitated before adding, "I guess I'll just worry about meeting your mom instead."

"I wish you wouldn't. She's going to love you."

In the shower together—which was quite tight because the chalet had certainly not planned for two men to use them for our purposes—we couldn't keep our hands to ourselves. Or our dicks, either.

God, I really loved Liam's cock in my ass.

When I shot my load down the shower drain, knees going weak with pleasure as Liam held me up, I didn't even care if my cry of satisfaction was overheard.

Being with Liam was just too damn good.

CHAPTER SEVENTEEN
Liam

I WAS SORE and tired after fucking North again in the shower. I was young and horny, sure, but four times in less than twelve hours was more than I was accustomed to, and we'd made each other come so many times the day before. I hadn't come that often since I was a teenager discovering what my cock could do.

My legs were shaky, my head was light, and I felt happier than I ever had in my life.

North was as tall as me, but he slouched as we got on the elevator, his hoodie pulled up to cover his head again. Apparently, the confidence of the afternoon before and the shamelessness he'd exhibited in the bed and shower had been all used up because as I pushed the button on the elevator down, he whispered, "How many people will be in the lobby area?"

"I don't know. We'll just have to see. Could be empty for all we know."

"Do you think your mom has seen it?" North asked.

I grappled with telling him the truth. I just didn't think it was a good idea for him to know—for sure—my mom had indeed seen his penis before we headed into Christmas celebrations. "There's nothing we can do about it if she has. Let's just take Ashton's advice and pretend she has and move on."

"I want to go back upstairs," North murmured. "I don't think I can do this."

I backtracked as the elevator reached the ground floor and

dinged before opening. "Then let's pretend she hasn't."

A small swarm of the other lodgers was in the lobby, and from the way they were wrapping scarves around their necks and stamping in their boots, I figured they were preparing to go to the farm next door for the horse-drawn sleigh rides offered to chalet guests.

I started to step out, but North balked.

"Okay?"

He just shook his head, and I slipped back onto the elevator, putting my arm over his shoulder and pulling him close. The doors slid closed, and we stood there in the quiet of the motionless elevator for a moment.

"I thought I could. I wanted to—no, I *want* to. Really, Liam. I want to go. A week ago, it would have been a dream to go with you to your mom's as your boyfriend but now? Now I don't think I can look her in the eye. She'll think you deserve better than someone dumb enough to put his dick online."

"North, this is—"

The elevator jolted and started moving up. Someone must have pushed the buttons from a floor above.

"Please don't say it's silly or stupid because this feels so big to me, Liam."

I huddled him nearer. "I know. I understand. But I promise you'll never meet a more loving woman than my mother. She'll want to bundle you up and hug you to death. She won't care at all about the picture."

I was pretty certain, at least.

"You're sure?"

"Yeah."

"And your sister?"

"She's not going to be upset about the picture either." Which was true. She held a grudge about the firing, but I wanted—no, *needed*—her to get over it. I needed my family to be there for North now and into the future because he was my very own love, and he deserved a family that wasn't half-jackal.

"Promise?"

"Promise."

The elevator stopped at our floor with a ding. Eric and the toilet-paper/coffee-pot guy, Max, boarded, with Eric so distracted he nearly plowed into me.

I noted how Max regarded Eric with fond amusement, and I couldn't help but say, "Well, I guess all that work hiding toilet paper and coffee pots wasn't for nothing."

Max laughed and hit the button for the ground floor. "No, except now he's acting like I'm dragging him to the gallows." He turned his gaze on his man. "It's only lunch, Eric."

Eric seemed tied into knots and didn't find the tease funny. "You don't understand. I can't go down there. There's a reason I never eat with the guests. Rhonda and Suzanne won't like it."

Max's brow wrinkled in confusion. He opened his mouth to speak, but I beat him to it.

"Bullshit," I said with a laugh. "Don't try to put this on Rhonda. She's not the reason you never mix with the guests." Eric had been avoiding socializing for years now. "Your exile has always been self-imposed. You know that."

Eric crossed his arms protectively and eyed me.

Max leaned his head toward North. "Speaking of self-imposed exiles, I notice yours is over?"

North went red but nodded, and I held him closer. Glancing up at me anxiously and probably wondering if Max and Eric had seen his dick—and they probably had—North seemed to be asking me to take over.

"Max and Eric, this is North. Eric, at least, has heard about him."

North cringed, imagining the worst, I was sure.

I shook him a little. "Not like that! I've *told* him about you."

"Many a conversation over beer," Eric confirmed.

"Oh." North looked up; his expression was still cautious, but he smiled. "I've heard about you, too. Liam has always talked about everyone here at the chalet as his second family."

"And this is Max, I presume," I said. "It's good to meet you. I've heard about you also."

The elevator dinged our arrival, but when the elevator doors opened, at least this time, North walked out with all of us. Peer pressure was good for something.

The car ride into Sandpoint with North was a quiet one.

I could tell he was still anxious despite my reassurances in the elevator. Occasionally, he'd comment on the sights and views. "The snow on the trees is so pretty," he said, pointing at the way snow hung like sugar-icing, coating every limb.

"Not missing the warm LA Christmas you're accustomed to?"

He reached out, still gazing out the window, to put his hand on my knee. "No. I'd rather be here with you."

"North?"

"Yeah?" he pulled his attention away from the views.

"These last two days have been cut out of real time, you know? And the next few will probably feel that way, too. But eventually, we need to come back to reality and figure out what we're going to do. What the next step is for us."

North sighed, running his hands through his hair, messing it up. His chin was still lightly shadowed even after his fresh shave, and I admired the cut of his jaw backlit by the window. He was so attractive. I wondered what he would be like when he was in his forties, and his insides were as mature as his outsides. I wanted to be in his life to find out.

"Where do you want to live?" North asked.

"Excuse me?"

"Do you want to live here? Near your mom? I can move here. The apartment in Seattle is worth more than enough for me to buy a house here, I'm sure. And if it's not. I have a trust."

"North—"

"Or do you want to live with me in Seattle? I've already told you I can help with the kids if childcare is unaffordable. I just want to be with you. Anywhere in the world. You name it. I'll make it happen."

"Baby…" I was shocked briefly into silence. I knew he felt this way, and I wanted to be with him anywhere in the world, too, but this wasn't a snap decision to make. "There are pros and cons to everything. We need to have some serious conversations about what we both want from our lives and make choices to help us get ourselves and each other there. We need to be strategic."

"What do you want from life?" North asked. "I've told you my dreams about the garden, but it's something I can make anywhere." He paused. "Plants grow everywhere, don't they? Except the desert? I vote we don't move to the desert."

My head was spinning. I concentrated on a tight squeeze around a curve downward before bringing my mind back to the conversation at hand. "What do I want from life?"

"Yeah. Like, I want to be with you, paint dragons, make a dragon garden, and after seeing those pictures of Ashton and Walker's dogs, maybe get a few of those. I miss Tyson."

"Oh."

"I mean, we don't have to get a dog if you don't want one."

"No, I like dogs," I said, my mind going in circles. *What do I want from life? What do I want…?* "It's just…"

"Wait, you do want to be with me, right?" North sounded panicked. "Southerland says I'm not good at reading what other people mean. Is this your way of saying—"

"Baby, you know I love you, and I want to be with you. I just realized I…" I stopped, ashamed to even say it out loud. After all,

166

North looked to me as a mentor of sorts, or at least he had in the past, and if I admitted this, he'd know the truth. In some ways, I was just as lost and confused about how to go forward with my life as he was.

"North?"

"Yeah." He was twisted in the seat to face me, his gaze following my every move. I could tell he was trying to read my mind. He was adorable doing it.

"I don't know what I want except I want you." I blinked rapidly. "I've been living these last few years on autopilot. First, I put my life on hold to watch the boys, and the pandemic shut everything down. Afterward, I just…kept on going like that. I didn't think to look toward the future. But now you're here, and I'm pretending like I know so much about everything. The truth is, I don't know what I want to change my life to look like or how I want it to be—except I know I want to add you."

"You can add me. I'll move here."

He said it easily.

"But what if I don't want to stay here? I know I don't want to watch my nephews for the rest of my life, doing tours in the summer and security gigs seasonally. I want some sort of *career* and *direction*."

"I'll be your direction," North offered.

"You'll be my north star?" I said, laughing and taking his hand in my free one.

"No, I'll be your North Pole." He grinned. "I'll be your forever trending topic."

I laughed and looked at him with some measure of awe. He was, as always, a surprise. I hadn't seen those jokes coming.

"But, really," North said. "We're both young. It's not like we have to know what we're doing with our lives right now, do we? That's what Grandma Ford tells me." He rolled his eyes. "Grandma Astor says it's not too late to enlist and let the military make a man of me. She says I'm too pretty to go to war. I don't know what she wants from me, but I don't think I'll ever get it right for her."

He was thoughtful now, but after a few beats, he turned back to me. "When you were a kid, what did you want to be when you grew up?"

"Superman," I said, with an embarrassed grin.

"You'd look good in that outfit." North shut his eyes. "I can see you in it." He licked his lips. I made a note for future role play if that got him hot. "But what else? Like after you realized you couldn't be Superman since he's an alien and all."

I chuckled, amused the problem was Superman was an alien and not that he was fictional. "I wanted to be a hero to someone. That's why I went into personal security work."

"You're my hero."

It was cheesy and ridiculous, but happiness surged inside.

North sat back, putting his hand on my knee again. "I think this is a problem which, as Southerland says, we can't solve in one day."

"That's what I mean. We have things to figure out before we can be together."

"No. It's fine. I'll just sell my apartment in Seattle and move here. I'll start planning the dragon garden thing, look for online classes on how to do it, or whatever. Plus, there's a lot of land around here for sale. I saw the signs." He nodded firmly. "I can start on it, and you can decide what you want from life as time goes by."

He made it sound so easy. Pragmatic almost, though it was all ridiculous and careless. Maybe even reckless.

"What if you do all that and it doesn't work out with us?" I asked.

"You just said you wanted to be with me always. Did you lie?"

"No, but wanting something doesn't make it happen."

"My dad has always said wanting something is ninety percent of the battle."

"Spoken like a rich man," I muttered.

"The other ninety percent is commitment and work."

"I don't think that adds up right."

North frowned at me. "You know math is my worst subject."

"Sorry." I laughed. "You know what?"

"What?"

"I've always loved how the chalet was a second home to me. I'd like to create a place that can be a second home to other people. Like a youth shelter or something or a foster home for teens. I remember reading about a guy from the band Vespertine—have you heard of them?"

"No."

"Well, the lead guitarist's partner runs a home for LGBTQ+ youth, and when I read about it, I felt inspired. I never knew how I'd ever be able to accomplish it, though, and I guess I still don't. But if I say that's what I want, I've won ninety percent of the battle, according to your dad."

"Right. And the other half is work and commitment."

I laughed.

"Keep in mind he's an actor, and all he does is pretend for a living."

I laughed again. "You're funny, you know?"

"I'm glad you think so." North smiled at me, and my heart sang. The trip to my mom's flew by as we continued to discuss our dreams for the future. By the time I pulled up into the driveway, North had nearly forgotten to be nervous.

Until he saw my mom step onto the front porch to greet us.

He turned to me and said, "Let's go back."

"No," I said. "We're going to stay."

North swallowed down his anxiety, took hold of my hand, and whispered, "You'll protect me?"

"I'll protect you always. You know that."

CHAPTER EIGHTEEN
North

L IAM'S MOM'S HOUSE was exactly what I'd expected it to be.
A family's actual home.

Not like the mansion I'd grown up in in California, which was more drama and bright glass than comfort and worn wood floors. Which was what Liam's house had. That and a Christmas tree with homemade decorations from Maeve's kids mixed in with purchased ornaments.

My mom's many matchy-matchy trees were always covered in ornaments priceless enough I was scared to walk by in case I knocked one off.

Liam's house also had fluffy rugs that'd seen better days and a worn-out sofa with a few stains on the cushions. Photos of family hung on the walls. And his house came with hugs. Lots and lots of hugs. Holy crap, I'd never had so many hugs before in my life, and definitely not in such a short period of time.

First from Liam's mom. Three times she'd hugged me before I'd even entered the house, throwing all my fear of her down the drain for good. Then from Liam's nephew Aiden, who was eager to climb me the way he climbed his uncle. Eventually, Liam had to pull him off.

From the baby, Jack, who "kissed" my cheek—which meant pressing his lips into a tiny, sticky pout and putting them against my face. He was adorable. I was willing to update my dream of the future to include a baby like him if Liam ever wanted to be a dad.

But Maeve's hug was cold.

Either she hadn't learned the Kelly way of embracing a person so it felt like they were being loved down to their very soul, or she hated me. I was pretty sure it was hate, given the hug she gave Liam. Though she also punched his shoulder, sent him a raised eyebrow, and said, "Really?" with as much disappointment and sarcasm as she could muster.

In that way, she reminded me of Southerland, which took a little of the edge off how scary I found her to be.

I was taken into their home like a long-lost family member, and as I was removing my shoes, I overheard Mrs. Kelly whisper to Liam, "He's a sweetheart. I can tell just by looking at him." She patted his arm like she was proud of him, like I was a catch. And not because of my money or my looks.

I wasn't sure how she'd seen my "good heart" from the outside already, but hearing her praise me felt nice.

After the greetings, Mrs. Kelly and Maeve excused themselves to the kitchen to check on the meal, with Jack toddling along behind them. Shortly, Liam followed, saying he'd be right back, leaving me with Aiden at my feet.

Padding through the house in just my socks, I felt out of place but also like I could eventually *find* my place here. It was familiar, different, strange, and right. It felt like the future calling to me. I decided to tell Liam later. He'd like that.

As the time ticked by without Liam in the room, Aiden urged me to come down to his bedroom to see his toys. I unclipped Jack and was surprised by how easy he was to hold. He clamped onto me like a little monkey. Aiden took hold of my hand and pulled us down to his bedroom, where Jack and I joined him on the carpet to drive cars around on the duct-taped racetrack on his floor. We raced and crashed them, and all got very wrapped up in the pile-up of all the cars we created by the bottom of his dresser.

Eventually, Liam found us. I didn't know how long he watched us from where he leaned in the doorway, but eventually, he cleared his throat, and I turned to see him there. Maeve wasn't far behind, her expression less cold than it'd been when I came in, but not entirely friendly either.

"You having fun?" Liam asked.

I laughed. "Believe it or not? I really am."

I'd never been able to play much in my youth. The enormous playroom I'd had was always chock full of toys and far too overwhelming. I'd never known where to start with it all. But here, with Aiden guiding me and telling me what to do with the cars, I was having a fantastic time. I could easily play this game with him again.

Liam said, "Lunch is late."

"At this point, it's drunch," Maeve said.

"Mom says it has about another forty minutes. In the meantime, we're going to play a game."

Aiden whined, but Maeve stepped in and took hold of his hand. "You can move my piece on the board, bud, okay?"

"I want to move North's piece."

"Well, that's up to North."

"Sure," I agreed, not knowing what I was committing to. "That's fine with me."

Maeve took Jack's chubby little hand as well, and the three of them left the room. Liam pulled me to standing, rubbed his fingers over my stubble, which was already starting to grow back in, and leaned in to kiss me. It wasn't sensual, just tender. Happy.

It was a happy kiss.

And I kissed him back.

"You're so undervalued in California," Liam murmured.

"I have an insurance policy on me for lots of millions of dollars," I assured him. "I'm valued at a lot."

"Oh, baby, that's not what I meant."

When I followed him out of the bedroom and into the hallway, I noted the photos on the walls. Mostly of him and Maeve, but there were a few of their whole family. Including one of them all in front of a waterfall. I paused, and Liam did too.

"Your dad?" I asked.

Liam's lips tilted up with a smile. It was the same smile as the man in the photo. "Yeah, that's him. He was, hmm, probably thirty-nine here? This is a good memory. One of the only trips we went on where Maeve and I didn't get in trouble for fighting."

Southerland and I didn't really fight. The way it worked with us was I said something, she told me I was an idiot, insulted me, and helped me think or say or do something better. But I knew most siblings fought a lot, and so far, Maeve gave me the impression she'd pick plenty of fights.

"He was handsome."

"Yeah," Liam agreed and took my hand again to pull me further down the hall into the living room. There I found a game of Clue set up and ready to go.

"This is the way we'll do it," Mrs. Kelly said. "We'll play Clue while the food finishes, and the winner gets the first serving of Christmas Eve supper."

"Supper, you see, because it's not lunch and it's not dinner, but it's in the afternoon, so Mom says supper, even though they are literally synonyms," Maeve explained.

"Ah," I said like I understood. "I like Clue."

"Are you good at it?" Aiden asked. "Because Mommy is da champ."

With those cool, dark eyes studying everything and everyone, I could well imagine she was. "I'm not good," I said. "But I'm not a sore loser."

"Let's hand out the pieces," Mrs. Kelly said, sitting cross-legged on the floor on one side of the coffee table. Each of the other three adults took a side, and Aiden crawled into Maeve's lap while Jack went back to playing with cars on the carpet near the tree.

"I'll be yellow," I volunteered. "Colonel Mustard." I smiled and murmured, "Thanks, Mrs. Kelly," as she handed over the piece.

"Oh, just call me Julie."

"All right. Julie." We grinned at each other, and I could see Liam's kindness in her, too. He'd gotten his smile from his dad, as I'd seen in the photo, but the red hair and freckles were from Julie. His dad had been black-headed and tan all over. Like Maeve.

The game went by in a flash, and I lost to everyone, including Aiden. They'd given him a piece to push around, even though he wasn't actually part of the game. He often yelled things like, "Miss Scarlet in the potty with a hairbrush," just to be funny. I laughed every time. So did Liam.

But I got the impression Liam was laughing at *me* for being cute. When it was over, Aiden declared himself the winner with Professor Plum in the kitchen with a snake, and no one bothered to argue with him.

We moved into the kitchen to eat our meal at the big table by a back window overlooking a fenced yard covered in thick snow. It was served buffet style, and we all took a plate and piled it high. The food was delicious and so incredibly common I almost cried with joy eating it.

There wasn't a single item with edible gold leaf, no White Alba truffles, no oysters or caviar. There was homemade gravy and mashed potatoes. There was a baked ham, a sweet potato casserole, and warm buns Maeve had made by hand and frozen in anticipation of the day. There were pies, too, and apparently, one of them was Liam's doing. Also made a week in advance and frozen to eat today.

I gasped as I took a bite of his apple pie. "You could be a baker!" I blurted out.

He grinned. "You could be my assistant. You could make dragon-shaped cakes."

"I wonder how hard that would be?" I asked, intrigued by the idea. It wasn't as enormous as a dragon-garden plan, but why couldn't I do both? "I've never baked a cake before. I'd be willing to try."

"Oh, then you'll have to come back and bake a cake with me," Julie said, her eyes flashing happily. "Won't he, Maeve?"

"Mom makes great cakes," Maeve said tightly, gaze running over me like she was trying to figure out a reason to keep hating me.

As we ate, the kids ate messily, played with their food, and eventually hopped down to go play cars in the living room again. The wine Julie served set us all more at ease, and I suddenly felt compelled to apologize to Liam's mom and sister for the past.

I didn't drink much anymore and never drank wine since it reminded me of my mother and her drinking issues, but I'd had two tonight, and now I was feeling maudlin. I felt like I was being allowed into a family experience I didn't deserve, hadn't earned, and might never get to have again unless I made it right with everyone in the room.

"I'm sorry," I blurted out as we all stood up to go to the living room again for the after-supper movie portion of the day. "I should never have fired Liam, and I'm sorry I did. I hope you can forgive me. I know it was bad timing, and you probably hate me for it, but—"

I took a quivery breath feeling even more emotional than I had before. "But I fell in love with him, and I had to fire him because it wasn't right, and I'd just turned eighteen, and it would have caused a big scandal. So I had to, and I hope you understand, and I'm sorry."

Liam shook his head and opened his mouth to speak when Maeve put her hand out to stop him. He shot her a warning look, but she didn't even see it. She had her eyes on me.

"Liam and Mom will both say you don't need to apologize, and maybe they're right because, well, with the way you look at each other—" she sighed. "You're in love, and I get how it would have ended very badly if he'd stayed around you back then. I get it now. But I also appreciate this apology from you, North because, yeah, it did put Liam in a bad way financially and career-wise. It was hard to watch him go through that."

"Maeve—" Liam started.

"I'm sorry," I repeated.

"Look, I'm glad you acknowledge and see what it cost him, even if, yes, it was the right thing to do. I appreciate you can admit to regret and to making mistakes. That bodes well for any relationship." She smiled, the warmest smile she'd given me yet. "Some people, like my ex, for example, are never able to do that. It says a lot about your character, and for the record, I forgive you."

"You do?"

"Sure." She grinned at me. "You'd rather I didn't?"

"I just want to be sure. I don't want to let my guard down and find you've poisoned my coffee. I mean, that happens sometimes. It happened to my dad's co-star's mother because she was being too annoying, and now that co-star's husband is in jail for murder. It was a Hollywood scandal."

"Wow."

My eyes went wide. I peered at my wine glass, realizing I wasn't sober. "Sorry. I didn't mean to, and I didn't have that much to drink. How?" I gaped at Liam. "It's the wine? I mean, I can drink *so much more* vodka than this."

He laughed. "It's okay. C'mon. *Die Hard* is waiting for us."

"*Die Hard?*"

"Only the best Christmas movie ever," Maeve said, leading the way into the living room, which was loud with vroom-vroom sounds and car crash noises from the boys.

While the other adults were setting up the streaming app for the movie, Aiden showed me how, if he ran just right, he could skid down the long hallway to the bedrooms in his socks. He urged me to try, and so I did, impressing him by skidding right into the bathroom door at the end of the hall. The door burst open, and I stumbled into the sink before I could stop myself. Luckily, the door was all right, even if my hip and ego were bruised.

"That's it!" Aiden shouted, pumping his fist. "Go North! You're da best!"

I came back into the living room flushed from exertion and embarrassment and was greeted with amused looks from the non-children in the room.

"Aiden loves you," Liam whispered, putting his arms around me, and pulling me close for a hug. "And so do I."

Liam and I were given the right half of the sofa for snuggling together, and Maeve and Aiden took the other half. Julie took the rocking armchair with Jack, and we had a bowl of popcorn each.

Aiden fell asleep against his mom's side well before Bruce Willis gave his famous yippee-ki-ay line, and Jack had been rocked into a sound sleep early on. I found it impossible to focus on the movie. My mind jumped from thought to thought.

I was here. With Liam's arm around me.

I was in his home with his mother and his twin sister. With his family.

They'd welcomed me here. I'd seen photos of his dad and a few of him as a baby and a child.

I'd left Seattle three days ago in shame and agony, and now, in this surreal moment, I was in a cozy, normal home in Sandpoint, Idaho, with a boyfriend who wanted me and encouraged me and with whom I might have a whole future full of dragon gardens, puppies, babies, baking, and maybe an LGBT+ youth retreat or something. I didn't know. But I wanted it all.

I'd been in love with Liam for so long. This all felt perfect.

It was home, family, love, and forgiveness. It was Christmas.

CHAPTER NINETEEN
Liam

"I GUESS WE'RE both just kids," North said suddenly on our way back to Camp Bay Chalet.

"Where'd that come from?" I asked, confused.

"I mean, you're older than me by three years, but both of us are just starting out in life. We're still figuring out how to be adults."

"Yeah, I guess you're right."

The snow was glistening in the lights from our car, and almost like a mirage, a *For Sale* sign flashed by us. North sat up straighter. "Did you see that?"

"The sign?"

"Yeah. We passed it right when I was talking about us figuring out how to be adults."

"North…"

He smiled at me, a bright, big smile. "Let's at least find out how much land it is. What if it's big enough for my dragon garden and your teen LGBT refuge or whatever? If we like it, I could buy it."

"That's a huge risk."

"No, it's not. For now, it's just looking," North pointed out.

I hesitated to agree. This was all moving fast. But I knew I wanted to be with North, and he wanted to be with me, and being close to my family was important to me, at least until the boys were grown. Just because I didn't want to be their full-time caregiver forever didn't mean I didn't want to be around to help out.

"All right," I agreed. "After Christmas, we'll have a look at it."

North's smile glowed in the dark of the car, lit up by the lights on the dash, and he grew quiet again until the decorations of the chalet came into view. He whistled under his breath. "So pretty. Like a fairy tale Christmas."

I had to agree. His gaze on the landscape of my childhood and youth gave me a new appreciation for it.

As we parked outside the chalet, I took hold of his hand, and we entered to find a whole lot of hubbub going on. In the lobby and library, cocktails were flowing, and so were words. Apparently, while we'd been out, there'd been an enormous drama with one of the guests at the lodge who'd turned out to have been stealing from the other guests. Shocking, to say the least.

"It was the most unChristmas-like thing I've ever experienced on Christmas," Olivia Powers said to the room at large, taking a gulp of her mulled wine.

"I don't know, it was definitely a gift to me," Ashton said, sauntering over with Walker at his heels. "There's nothing like drama to pep up a party, and this one had been getting a little dull right before the big reveal went down."

Eric, it seemed, had been traumatized by it all, and Max was off trying to soothe him.

After we'd been fully informed about the dramatic and illegal events going on in the chalet for the last few days, we headed into the sitting room to share in the eggnog, desserts, and other munchies. There was a big fire roaring in the library, and I asked North if he wanted to ditch the crowd and hang out there for a while.

But North had other plans. He drew me into the event room, where a local band was playing lively Christmas tunes. It was a Celtic sort of sound, with flute and strings, and it made me want to dance.

"You want to?" North asked, tugging me toward the dance

floor. "When you were protecting me, I used to fantasize about dancing with you at all my parents' parties."

"No pressure." I chuckled. "Just fulfilling a fantasy here and all. But what if I'm a terrible dancer?"

North grinned. "Then we can be terrible together."

He wasn't lying. He wasn't light on his feet, but when the flutist took a break, and the music changed to a slow and sexy rendition of "Jingle Bell Rock," it didn't matter anymore.

Pressed against him, swaying back and forth, breathing in his scent, and rubbing our noses together, nothing had ever felt this right.

"You think everyone's so into talking about this big crime drama tonight that no one's looking at me and thinking about my dick?"

I glanced around the room, and yes, people were still gossiping and chatting. Not a soul was watching us on the dance floor. "I'm not sure *everyone* is distracted from your dick, but most folks seem to be, yeah."

North's brow wrinkled. "You think someone's still thinking about my dick?"

"For sure."

"Who?"

"Me."

North laughed.

When the song ended, and the flutist returned to the stage, North took hold of my hand and tugged me off the dance floor, saying, "I heard someone saying earlier there were still horse-drawn sleigh rides available. Let's do one."

I wanted to suggest we go upstairs and slow dance naked together, but his eyes were bright with interest, and I decided nakedness could wait.

For a while, anyway.

Besides, it would be fun to warm North up again back in the room after a cold, snowy sleigh ride.

THE SLEIGH WAS cozy. We were tucked beneath blankets at the back, and the driver sat well ahead of us on a separate, higher bench, guiding the horses through the white, moonlit wonderland around us. The lake was beautiful in the night, reflecting the moon and the stars while also seeming to ripple with a light of its own.

The blankets were thick and warm but not entirely soft. A little scratchy. Still, I was feeling snug as a bug in a rug next to North as the horses clopped into the forest, cutting off our view of the night sky. The scent of pine and wet earth rose, as well as the crisp, sharp scent of snow.

I didn't *decide* to kiss North; it just happened. He was beautiful in the moonlight, his dark hair gleaming, his cheeks pink with cold, and his gorgeous mouth opening over every break in the trees, which showed off a view of the lake and the mountains.

First it was a simple peck, and then it turned into open-mouthed soft kisses. Soon I couldn't resist the way he squirmed and responded to my every touch. Before long, we were necking and kissing like horny teenagers.

North's hands got busy under the blanket, rubbing over my legs and crotch, getting me hard. I gave as good as I got, and when he was so aroused he couldn't keep from making needy little noises, I unbuttoned and unzipped his jeans, working my hand inside. North tensed, his gaze going to the driver, but, as usual with sleigh rides, the man never turned his head, keeping his attention on the horses and the forest trail ahead.

"Good?" I whispered as I pumped him slowly.

North's eyes gleamed, and he nodded. His mouth fell open, and puffs of air released from between his red lips. I kissed him again, tonguing his sensitive places and pulling his plump bottom lip into my mouth. Pulling back to peer into his face, watching every nuance of moonlit expression crossing it, I looked for the moment when need crushed out everything else.

He was going to come. Good God, this was much more than I could have *dreamed* of even a year ago.

Me and North.

My hand on his dick.

My lips on his.

As the sleigh rounded another curve, I felt dizzy with love and joy. The world around us condensed to this sleigh, this moment. The wind in my hair and the tangle of his tongue were blissful. The world was us, and we were the world, the wind just another way for us to love and stroke each other, and the blankets extensions of our hot bodies.

The peak came quickly. I was torn between holding him off and letting him ride it out now. The incandescent glow of his eyes, the redness of his lips, and the way he whispered, "Please," made up my mind. I checked the driver was still focused on his job before lifting the blanket, and ducking below to suck the head of North's cock into my mouth.

It was only a matter of a few fast pumps, some good suction, and excellent use of my tongue before North's hips bucked up and cum filled my mouth. I drank it down, licking his shaft to get every bit. I emerged from the darkness beneath the blankets, back into the cold of the night. My tongue tingled, my lips were slick, and I kissed him again.

North melted into me, his hand tentatively returning to my crotch to reciprocate, but I pushed his questing fingers away. "No. I'm saving it for later. In our room."

North nodded, snuggling me close, and we spent the rest of the snowy ride basking in the afterglow. When we got back to the inn, there would be fireworks over the lake. The gifts just kept coming, and Christmas joy went on and on.

CHAPTER TWENTY
North

December 25

THE NEXT MORNING, I woke to the tinny sound of a toddler crying and an excited child's voice. Rolling over, I saw Liam was on FaceTime with Aiden, who was proudly showing him the candy he'd received in his stocking from Santa.

I smiled, my mind flashing back to my own childhood and Southerland and my excitement on Christmas morning. The toys, the junk food, and the way my parents were blasted drunk on Bloody Marys by noon.

Those had been good times because while my parents were chaotic when intoxicated, they were often warmer and more fun than when they were sober. There was a reason they were dependent on the alcohol, after all. They joked it made them more "human," but they weren't far off the mark.

"Merry Christmas, buddy," Liam said, his voice scratchy with sleepiness. "It seems like Santa was good to you this year."

"When will you be home?" Aiden's small voice asked.

Liam glanced my way before saying, "Probably tomorrow. I'm not sure. But I'm going to see you today when you all come to Camp Bay Chalet for the Christmas party, remember?"

"I 'member," he muttered, sounding like that might not be good enough.

The phone was passed around, with greetings from Maeve, a shout from Jack, and a blown kiss from his mother. But the call only ended when Aiden had extracted a promise from Liam to help Maeve build the new outdoor playhouse Santa had brought on the very day he returned.

After disconnecting, Liam turned to me, his expression serious. "Okay, your turn."

"For what?" My mind immediately went to the sex we'd had the night before, and I wondered if he wanted me to top him.

"To call your family."

I drew back. "Why?"

"It's Christmas morning." Liam checked his watch. "They'll be up by now. Mrs. Astor will be making those pancakes with the chocolate chips for Southerland and mixing her third Blood Mary by now."

"You know them really well."

"Your parents are a lot of things, and predictable is definitely one of them. Especially when it comes to family time. I know they're difficult, but they do value the time with you and Southerland. I saw that when I was there. They'll be missing you."

"They told me not to come home."

"They didn't. You decided not to go home because you didn't want to."

I sat up, letting the blankets fall away, and shivered in the cool air. Stepping toward the fireplace, I flipped the switch to start the gas fire and grabbed a robe. Liam stood and pulled on some sweats, a T-shirt, and socks.

When we were both not naked anymore, I took up my cell phone and put through a FaceTime to my family. Better to get it over with.

"Darling!" Mom's voice was cheerful, and sure enough, she was swilling a bright red drink and standing in the kitchen, probably making the pancakes. "I was hoping you'd call."

I didn't mention she had my number and could have called me

herself because it seemed pointless. Liam looked at me expectantly. This was a Christmas Day making-nice moment, not a time for being petty. "Merry Christmas."

"And Merry Christmas to you, too!"

A taut voice snapped, "Let me talk with him."

I gaped at Liam, dread filling me. Grandma Astor wanted to talk with me? I'd known she'd be there for the day, but I'd hoped she wouldn't arrive until later. If I had to talk to any grandmother, I'd hoped to talk to Grandma Ford, who lived in the house. But instead, I was faced first with my fire-breathing grandparent.

"North, what are your plans to make this humiliation up to your family?" Grandma Astor was dressed for breakfast, wearing pearls and a matronly red dress.

"Mother," Mom said in the background. "It's Christmas. Be nice."

"At least you didn't shame us by having a small one, but I'd like to know how you plan to salvage your reputation. Charity work is a good start. I have a list of fine organizations that will be happy to have you on board. When you return tomorrow—you are coming home tomorrow, aren't you?—we'll sit down and choose one. It can't have anything to do with children, obviously, or gay rights. You've made enough of a mess without reminding everyone you're a pansy—"

"Mother Astor!" Dad's irritated voice came through loud and clear. "We don't use words like that in this house."

I sat in silence, gazing at Liam, just letting the chaos of my home life unfurl into the room like a wave. Liam pressed his lips together, and, damn him, he looked as if he might laugh.

"All right, fine. But we don't need to remind the world the boy is an LGBT. Isn't that the proper term?"

"No," I said as my mom and dad also said no in the background.

"Well, regardless. When you get home, see me. We'll fix this."

The phone was passed unceremoniously to my dad, whose handsome face filled the screen. His gaze followed Grandma Astor before he turned to face me. "Son! Merry Christmas! Your mother is making the traditional chocolate chip pancakes. We're sorry you're not here to eat them with us."

I didn't mention they hadn't tried very hard to get me to come home, but instead, I reassured them I was getting plenty of good things to eat. "The chalet offers great pastries in the mornings."

"And Liam? Is he with his family this morning?"

"He's here. With me."

My father's face broke into a sunny smile. "Fantastic. He's a good young man. He'll keep you on track."

Dad's comment seemed to strike Liam negatively for a moment. He clenched his jaw before releasing it and smiling gamely again at me.

"He will," I agreed.

"Not that I agree with Grandma Astor—"

"Heaven forbid you ever agree with a word I say," her voice called out.

"But when can we expect you home? And what are your plans after this?"

I was tempted to say I was never coming home again for the rest of my life, and I'd found a small community here where people didn't hold things like my dumb brain or my big dick against me and where I didn't have to pretend to be anyone or anything but myself.

Instead, I said, "Maybe I'll come home for New Year's Eve." I glanced at Liam, whose brows had slipped into a frown. "Or maybe not. I like it here in Camp Bay."

Dad's eyebrows furrowed, much like Liam's. "What's there to do in Idaho, son? Better to come home and let us help you get your life arranged again. We can sell or rent the apartment in Seattle—real estate is always a profitable investment there—and you can—"

"I don't think so," I interrupted him. "I mean, yes, let's sell the apartment. I want the money to buy land here in Camp Bay."

Mom wrangled the phone out of Dad's hand, peering into the screen with bright eyes which said the Bloody Marys had contained a lot of vodka. "What would you do with *land*, sweetheart?"

I hesitated because my parents always thought my dragon and alien art fascination was ridiculous, but I went ahead and told the truth. What else was there to say? "I want a place to make art and also to learn to cultivate a garden."

"Gardens are more easily cultivated in California," Dad said.

"I like the winter," I said. "I like the snow."

"And Liam is in Camp Bay," Mom said knowingly. "Well, darling, we could move him here. Set him up with a nice apartment while you figure out if you work as a couple, and—"

"That's nice, Mom, but his family is here."

"Your family is *here*," Dad said.

I bit my lip to keep from reminding them that a few days ago, I'd been an embarrassment. My parents were always full of mixed messages. "California is always there," I said carefully, trying to think of how Liam might phrase things. "It's not like if I stay here for a while, I can't ever come home."

"No," Mom agreed reluctantly. "It doesn't mean that."

"Mm, I smell pancakes!" Southerland's voice cut in. "Are you talking to North?" Her face appeared, squeezing in at the edge of the screen. "Hey, Merry Christmas."

"Merry Christmas," I replied.

"You look happy," she said, narrowing her eyes and pushing Dad over so she could get more space on the screen. "Or something."

I smiled shyly, shrugging. "I am happy."

Mom and Dad shared a significant look, and they both capitulated at once. "Send us more information about this land you're interested in. There's an airport nearby, surely. We could come up for ski vacations, too. This will work out."

I blinked. I hadn't realized my happiness was of any importance to them. I always thought it was about reputation and appearances, but at the mention of my own personal happiness, they'd both changed their tune without hesitation. I glanced toward Liam. He seemed unsurprised.

"How are things with Liam?" Grandma Ford asked when she joined the family call wearing her blue silk robe Dad had gotten for her with his first acting paycheck all those years ago.

I was relieved she didn't mention the picture scandal or seem at all ashamed of me. I should have known better, but still, the idea she'd seen that picture burned through my mind, and I blushed.

She ignored it, if she noticed at all. "Is he still the good boy he used to be?"

"Yes, how's Liam?" Mom called from where she'd apparently gone back to making pancakes for Southerland.

"Good. He's here," I said. "And, yeah, he's still good." I blushed even more.

"Let me talk with him," Grandma Ford said. "Put him on."

Liam came closer to me, and we squeezed in together so his face was on the screen, too.

"There you are, young man. The boy my North ran off to find when things got hard."

A large silence seemed to consume the pause before her next sentence, making it heavy with meaning I knew she didn't intend.

Liam pinched his own leg in a clear attempt not to laugh.

I pinched him, too, and he straightened his face up quickly.

"You were always a good boy. I remember how you watched after him, thought ahead about how to help him, and would make him bacon and avocado sandwiches in the middle of the night."

"It was just once," Liam said, chuckling. "He was hungry."

"And perfectly capable of making the food himself, but you took care of him instead. I appreciated you back then, and I know my son and Susan did, too."

"I didn't," Grandma Astor said in the background. "He always seemed fruity to me, but now we know he *is*, so... I was right. He's an LGBT."

"No, that's not how you say it," Dad said.

"Whyever not?"

"It's just...not."

"Well, what do you say?"

"Labels don't matter," Dad said loftily. "He's our son's boy-friend, and isn't that good enough?"

Grandma Astor snorted, and on screen, Grandma Ford rolled her eyes. "We know North is safe with you."

"And I'm safe with North," Liam said. "We'll take care of each other."

"Yes, you're both good boys. Young and in love." She smiled fondly.

"All right, well, we should go down for breakfast before all the best pastries are gone," I said, hoping to put an end to all this weird, schmoopy business.

The family crowded onto the screen, save Grandma Astor, who wouldn't be caught crowding in any situation, and Southerland offered my send-off. "Merry Christmas, idiot. You got lucky with Liam. I hope you appreciate that." She laughed, catching her accidental double meaning. Slinking away from the phone, she shouted, "Oh my God, why is this my life?"

My parents and Grandma Ford wished me a happy day, and Mom said, "Whatever makes you happy, whoever makes you smile like this, we support it, darling."

I nodded, dazed, as I ended the call. I hadn't expected them to put up a fuss over Liam exactly, but I hadn't expected them to give in so easily to my Camp Bay plans and the relationship responsible for them.

"They love you," Liam said, once I'd wished them all a Merry Christmas again, endured another few awkward moments with Grandma Astor, and been loved up by Grandma Ford one last time. "They're strange about how they show it, but they want you to be happy."

"But usually, they want me to be happy with what *they* want me to be happy with."

"I'm just grateful they trust I can be part of your happiness."

"Me too." Liam meant enough to me that if my parents *did* fight my relationship with him, I'd refuse to back down, but I was grateful they supported what we had.

"Now, let's get ready and head down for those pastries. Suzanne also fixes up some mean bacon."

CHAPTER TWENTY-ONE
Liam

"ARE YOU FEELING better?" I asked after we'd gone down to breakfast, eaten with Ashton and Walker again, and headed back upstairs to snuggle and nap. The urgency of the prior days seemed to be slipping into more of a feeling of comfort and joy, though the heat was always there, ready beneath the surface to surge up and swallow us for a few sexy hours.

"Yeah, I was pretty hungry."

"No, I mean about the incident with the picture."

North went still before he sighed. "I think I'll probably always be embarrassed about it, but it feels safe here in the chalet. You were right. The people here don't seem to care too much. Even the guy at the front desk—"

"Sal."

"Yeah, even he seems to be over it."

"It's old news to him, I'm sure."

"I wish it hadn't happened, but I don't want to spend the rest of my life thinking about it. There are more exciting things to focus on now."

"Like?"

"Like calling that phone number on the sign we saw to ask about buying some land."

"We should do plenty of due diligence before we sink money into anything."

"That's fine."

"I like imagining it, though. You and me, in our own place, an art studio set off and away from the house, but with a view of the lake, too."

"You've been picturing details? Me too. I'll have a garden. I'll start small. The big dragon plan will have to wait until I see if I can even make plants grow."

"That's wise."

"But I keep seeing big dragons wrapped around mountainsides, breathing steam over a big lake. I could paint that."

"You could."

"Maybe I could sell it."

"You could."

"And you'll start working with some contractors to build the shelter for LGBTQ+ youth."

"There's a lot to consider before I ever get that far."

"But you want to?"

"I mean, it'd be a dream."

"You could talk to that guy, the one who dates the guitarist in that band."

"Vespertine."

"Yeah. I bet he could help you."

"How would I even meet him?"

"My dad is Deacon Ford, remember? His people will call Vespertine's people." North shrugged. "Then you have a meeting."

"Just like that?"

"Yeah."

My head swam, trying to imagine meeting with Nico Blue from Vespertine and his lover Jasper Hendricks, talking with them about their passion for youth outreach, especially LGBTQ+, and discussing what we could do in the Camp Bay area.

In Idaho, in general, really. There had to be all kinds of legalities involved. Things I didn't even know to consider. Right now, all of it had seemed above my head, but with North's family's help, it could be a *real* dream, not just a fantasy.

"I never let myself think it was possible before."

"Let's think about it," North said. "Let's start living our dreams. I've spent way too much time being worried about what they'll write about me in the gossip columns. Now they've all seen my dick, and now I'm with you because of it, so maybe it doesn't matter anymore. If people think painting dragons is stupid, that's okay with me. I still want to do it."

"What will you do in the meantime?" I asked. "There's a lot of room between the here and now and the dreams you want to live."

"What do you mean?"

"Like where will you live, North? Tomorrow, the day after that? Where will you be?"

"I want to be with you."

I snuggled him close. "I want that, too. But my mom's house is already crowded."

North held me, thinking hard. I could feel his brain working.

"I'll move in here. Rhonda, Suzanne, and the rest won't mind if I live here for a year or two while we work things out, will they? So long as I pay?"

I blinked. The thought had never occurred to me. The chalet had always been a short-term place for people to vacation, but there was no real reason North couldn't stay longer. He'd fit in well here. I had no doubt Rhonda and Suzanne would make him family in short order. And he'd be safe. No one at the chalet would let anything bad happen to him. And he'd be close. I could even stay with him often.

"Is that what you want?"

"Yes."

"How can you be sure?"

"Because I've never really wanted anything before. I didn't want the apartment in Seattle, or to go to college, or to be kissed by Robson Reynolds. I didn't want to live in California or go to boarding school. But I wanted you from the moment I saw you. And now I want this. I feel it in my gut. These are the choices *I* want to make. Everything before this has been someone else's idea. This one is mine."

I kissed the top of his head. He was young—we both were—and we were sure to make a lot of foolish mistakes, and maybe these dreams of ours would end up being just that. But maybe they wouldn't be.

I couldn't wait to find out.

CHAPTER TWENTY-TWO
North

THE CAMP BAY Chalet Christmas Day party was well attended. All the guests showed up, and most of the employees and their families did as well. I still didn't know everyone from the chalet well, but I liked everyone I'd met, and when I brought up a longer-term residence, Rhonda's smile was so warm I felt at home immediately. I knew I'd made the right choice.

"You won't get bored here?" Suzanne asked, standing next to the big fireplace warming her backside. "It's a slow, sleepy town. The kids who grow up here are always anxious to get out. It won't be what you're accustomed to."

"I've never liked the lifestyle I grew up with. Too many people, too many parties. I want to slow down and meet people who aren't interested in the latest gossip or all that Hollywood stuff."

"Well, there is Sal," Suzanne said, laughing.

Jerome chuckled.

Liam said, "North wants to buy some land, too, to build a home and to work on art."

"Art?"

"Dragons," I said, lifting my chin, determined not to be embarrassed. This woman had seen a picture of my hard dick; she could deal with my artistic inspirations, no matter how odd or juvenile they might seem.

"Dragons! I love it. So specific," Rhonda said. "You know what? There's an old shed out near the equipment shed. It's in need of a good cleanup, but if you were to be the one to tackle it, you could set up out there to pursue your art as long as you're staying here with us."

"You would allow that?"

"Sure. It's not as if it's being used anyway."

"We can talk about the details later," Suzanne said with a friendly pat on my arm. "Let's get back to the kitchen. There are snacks to replace."

Liam's family arrived shortly after eleven. Aiden ran to him and climbed him like a tree until Liam swung him up to sit on his shoulders. This meant Aiden had to duck low over Liam's head every time they walked into a new room, which the boy found giggle-inducingly delightful.

The party had all sorts of activities—dancing, cookie decorating, a Santa experience for the kids, crafts, cocktails and hot cocoa, and sleigh rides again. At first, we stayed close to Liam's family, taking Aiden and Jack through the line to sit on Santa's lap and helping them play a game of Santa cornhole. Jack tried to imitate his brother, even though he was an unsteady walker still.

I loved being at Liam's side, watching and helping with the children.

It was unbelievable to me. Not even a week ago, I had no idea this could exist. Or that I could be here with Liam's mom and sister and his nephews and be treated like one of the family.

When I'd punched the name into my GPS, I'd had no idea Camp Bay Chalet would change my life. I'd come here to hide and be ashamed, and instead, it had woken me to a whole new future.

"Baby," Liam called, motioning me over. "What do you say to another sleigh ride?" His smile sparkled, and my heart skipped a beat.

"In the daytime?"

He nodded.

"All right."

He took my hand, drew me near, and kissed my lips. "Let's go."

"Yes."

In the glistening shadows of the woods, I got out my iPhone and took another selfie of the two of us. Our eyes looked like stars, and our cheeks were flushed with cold and excitement. I gazed at the photo, took a deep breath, and whispered, "Are you ready?"

"If you are."

I opened my Instagram Story and posted the photo of the two of us, adding a blinking sticker reading LOVE in a bright pink font. I sent it through, and in a rush, notifications came in from Facebook, Twitter, and everywhere else I had an account. The automatic cross-post was still set up.

But this time, instead of the cold chills of horror, I felt the hot thrill of delight. It was Christmas Day, a time of new beginnings for the world. This was *my* new beginning as Liam's boyfriend, as someone aside from "North Astor-Ford of the Astor-Ford hotel-and-acting fortune."

"Can you imagine the gossip sites' clickbait headlines?" I murmured as he and I watched the flood of incoming good wishes and expressions of disgust. The usual mix.

"North Astor-Ford and his new man heat up Christmas," Liam offers.

"North Astor-Ford and his red-headed hunk take a sleigh ride into love."

"North-Astor Ford's new hot slice of Gingerbread."

Remembering the trending hashtag, I waggled my eyebrows. "North's Pole has a hot new hole."

Liam's expression softened. "More like North's Pole has found a new home."

"Home? Is this—" I motioned between us. "Our home?"

Liam smiled. "Isn't it?"

"Yes," I replied, breathless.

"When we get back, let's say goodbye to my family and go upstairs."

"Yeah? Why?"

"Because, baby, I've got a home for your pole right here."

I laughed. He laughed. The comments kept coming in, but none of them mattered. Neither would the headlines when they appeared. And if the paparazzi showed up tomorrow, we'd find a way to deal with them. I loved Liam, and he loved me.

Later, after the party was over, after we'd said goodbye to his family, warned them about possible paparazzi calls, and told Ashton and Walker so long, we were finally alone again in our room.

"I'm going to have to go back to Seattle for a few days," I said. "I need to get my stuff and arrange to sell the apartment."

"I'm going to miss you."

"I know; I'll miss you, too."

We were naked in bed and trying not to end things too soon. He kissed my neck, and I held my hips away from his so we wouldn't go too far, too fast. "You know what?"

"What?" he asked, his voice muffled since his face was buried in my armpit now, sniffing me there. I wasn't ticklish, but it still felt strange and intimate. I loved letting him do whatever he wanted to me.

"I want to spend every Christmas here from now on."

"Mm?" He licked my armpit hair and made a face. "Tastes like deodorant."

I laughed. He moved on to kissing my nipples, which was a lot more distracting. I kept my focus, but barely. "Don't you want to stay here for Christmas every year? Even if we have our own house?"

"Maybe," he said, going up on his elbows above me. His red hair was a mess, and his face was flushed beneath his freckles. "I think we could spend Christmas Day here from time to time, as an anniversary sort of thing. But once we're in our own place, we might want a private, quiet holiday there."

"I guess we'll see."

"Yeah." Liam grinned. "We'll see."

I licked my lips. Liam was so beautiful, and I needed him so much. In every way possible. He was my home. Remembering our joking hashtags, an idea came to me, new and surprising. "Liam?"

"Yeah, baby?"

"I never thought I'd be asking for this. To be honest, I didn't even know I wanted it until just now." I laughed. "It's strange because it's never even seemed very appealing before, but with you…"

"What do you want?"

"Can I fuck you?"

He rubbed his nose against mine and sat up, reaching for the lube on the bedside table. "Of course. I am and have always been at your service." He said it as a tease, but I knew it was true.

It was only a few minutes later I pushed into him for the first time. Liam's head fell back, his throat convulsing as I slid in deeper. "Baby…" he whispered. "You're so big. Holy shit. Ungh." He grunted, struggling to take me all the way.

"Do you want me to stop? Does it hurt?"

Liam shook his head. "No, I can handle it. But, damn, *hashtag North's Pole*."

I laughed, but as I kissed him, grateful tears filled my eyes. My heart had never known this much joy could exist.

Liam whispered to me as I began to thrust, words of encouragement, words of affection, promises, and vows.

I whispered those back.

Somewhere in the house, the sound of Christmas bells began to chime. I didn't know if it was real or all in my mind, a hallucination brought on by happiness. It didn't matter. As I crested into orgasm,

Liam drew me into a heated kiss. Collapsing on him, I trembled as his arms came around me, holding me close and safe forever.

This was love, and I was going to make it my new home and live in it with Liam always.

EPILOGUE
Liam

Three years later

THE PAPARAZZI FOLLOWED us whenever we visited North's family in California.

Over time, I got used to seeing my picture online and in grocery store tabloids. Usually, they had nothing negative to say about either of us, aside from jabs at our "hideous" style choices. The idea that maintaining up-to-the-minute fashion didn't fit our Idaho lifestyle didn't seem to register with them.

The only scandalous accusation came last month when we were in LA for Thanksgiving. North accidentally tripped and splashed his latte all over me as we walked from a Starbucks near our hotel to our car.

He'd cried, "Now we're going to be late!" when he'd realized we'd have to return to our room for me to change. We'd been on our way to attend a lecture from Serenah Prince, one of the top garden designers in the world. North was a huge fan of hers. He had started attending online classes in horticulture last year and was still working on his dragon-garden plans, and Serenah's design styles and how she integrated support of the local flora and fauna into them were a huge inspiration. He'd been looking forward to her lecture for months, so, of course, he was upset.

The hungry LA paparazzi had been looking for something, *anything* negative to report on us for such a long time, and they decided they finally had their chance. They spun the photos and video they'd grabbed, claiming North had purposely thrown the coffee on me in a fit of rage for making him late. *North Astor-Ford's Thanksgiving Tantrum* was the headline they ran with.

"I would never throw coffee on you," North had moaned, stressed about the lies.

"Of course, you wouldn't," I'd soothed.

The Astor-Fords' attorneys suggested he rebut the accusation, but I'd told him to forget about it. We both knew what'd happened, and anyone who knew North even a little would never believe he'd throw coffee at an *ant*, much less the man he loved.

I hoped it was the last time the media picked on North, but I was sure it wouldn't be.

Thankfully, three years after the cross-posting mistake that'd brought North into my arms, *Hashtag North's Pole* had been relegated to the back of people's minds, a dusty memory of an enormous honky-honk (as my mother insisted on calling my nephews' privates.) In the endless stream of fraught celebrity scandals, North's penis couldn't keep a foothold in the minds and hearts of fickle fans and Tweeters.

But he and his dick had a hold on me like no other.

We sat on the deck of our newly expanded Tiny House (Medium House) built on the property he'd seen during the drive back from my mom's place on our first Christmas Eve as a couple.

It'd turned out to be the perfect price, with plenty of room for multiple small buildings, all of which served different functions: an art house, a tool shed, a storage unit, a gardening shed, and a greenhouse. As well as a small barn big enough for three horses. He wanted us to learn how to ride.

We were on our outdoor sofa, cleaned of snow and covered with the pillows we usually kept in the storage unit during the winter. We'd bundled up tightly in thick blankets, leaving one hand free to hold our wine glasses as we cuddled and waited for the fireworks to begin over Lake Pend Oreille. Our neighbors, Camp Bay Chalet, put them off every year on Christmas Eve at precisely nine o'clock.

"You happy, baby?" I asked North, leaning my head to rest against his shoulder. Somehow, he'd filled out a bit more over the last few years, and now he was broader than me.

"Yeah," North replied, his breath frosty. It was seriously cold. The snows had come early this year. The world around us was packed in white snow, beautiful and freezing. "You?"

"Of course."

"Even though the county didn't approve your LGBTQ+ Youth Center plan?"

I sighed. "It's disappointing, but I didn't expect to have an easy time of it. Jasper warned me *any* queer center or organization was going to face pushback. I haven't given up."

For the last three years, thanks to North's dad's connections, I'd had regular video meetings with Jasper Hendricks, the partner of Vespertine's guitarist. He'd taught me a lot about how to get my vision nailed down and make a start at it. He'd even asked his lawyers to work with the attorneys North's parents had engaged for me. He told his people to pass on everything they'd learned about setting the organization up properly.

"You'll never give up," North agreed. "Even if we have to go somewhere else to do it. You're a hero, and heroes don't quit."

I smiled again, touched as always by his faith in me. "I don't want to go anywhere else, though. That's the problem."

"We *have* made a good home here, haven't we? Away from the world. No media, no Hollywood bullshit. Only your family and our Camp Bay family. And here, in our house, I love how it's just you and me, and doggie makes three."

"Speaking of, where's Samantha?" I hadn't seen our twelve-year-old rescue Golden retriever since we came outside. "She'll be scared when the fireworks start."

"Asleep by the fire. She was too cute to wake up just to come outside to freeze with us."

North's phone buzzed, and he almost dropped his wine trying to answer the FaceTime call from Southerland.

"Hey, you lucky jerk," Southerland said as soon as the call connected. She wore her hair in an updo and had applied tasteful makeup. The fancy-schmancy dress she had on made it plain she hadn't been able to escape the Astor-Ford parties this year.

"Having fun?" North asked.

"No."

"Should have taken my suggestion to come stay at the chalet. The Christmas Day events there are fun, and Suzanne's dinners are the most comforting, down-home meals ever. Plus, Liam's mom is dying to meet you."

"That's sweet of her," Southerland said genuinely. "Maybe I'll come up next year. Where are you right now? It's really dark; I can barely see you."

"On the deck, waiting for the Christmas fireworks to start."

"Where's Liam?"

North moved his screen so I was in the shot, too.

"Oh, good," Southerland said, feigning relief. "I was afraid you'd finally run him off with your special brand of st—" She stopped herself.

I'd made it clear to the family that no one, and I meant *no one*—not even me—would ever call North stupid or dumb or idiotic again.

She re-worked her sentence. "Your special brand of annoying."

"Never. He's stuck with me," North said. "Because *he* thinks my special brand of *everything* is super hot."

She gagged.

"Why didn't you come up?" I asked. Though inwardly, I was glad. I liked taking North apart in every single room of the house, letting him feel my deep love for him on every surface and every rug. Hard to do that when my soon-to-be sister-in-law was around.

"Well, I *might* sort of kinda have a date for the parties this year," she said shyly.

"Who?" North demanded, puffing up with brotherly protection. It was adorable.

"You don't know him."

"Tell me anyway. Who?"

"Alec Riley."

North's shoulders relaxed. "Oh. I never met him, but his sister's pretty nice. I kissed her in a closet once back in high school. She didn't try to take advantage."

"The backward cliché of kissing a girl in a closet and a boy at the altar," Southerland said with a giggle.

"Not until next fall," I said. The thought of marrying North by Lake Pend Oreille as the autumn leaves drifted down in oranges, reds, and yellows made my heart sing.

"Still, you know what I mean." Glancing over her shoulder, she sighed. "Alec isn't here yet, though. What if he doesn't come?" She bit into her lower lip, looking vulnerable. It was sweet to see her turn to her big brother for help. She so rarely did.

"Then he's an idiot," North muttered. "You're amazing. You should only be with people who recognize that." He glanced at me. "Like Liam and I do."

"Yeah," Southerland agreed. Another heavy sigh. "Well, I should go. Mom's been in the vodka all day, so she's being messy, and Dad's already downing manhattans like they're sugar-free colas."

"And Grandma Astor?" I couldn't resist asking.

"Bitching about the floral arrangements, *and* the china, *and* the new-money guests, *and* my hair."

"What's wrong with your hair?"

"It's too mine," she laughed. "Come home, North. Come be her punching bag for me until the new year."

"Sorry, the only person who gets to hit North is me, and that's only in the sexy way." I mimed a spanking.

"Ew."

North laughed.

Somewhere behind Southerland, a door must have opened because suddenly, party noises poured over the connection. Looking over her shoulder again, Southerland raised her hand, indicating one minute. Turning back, she waved. "Gotta go, but everyone sends their love."

"Tell them I love them, too," North said. "So does Liam."

I was learning to forgive North's family for their deep, deep flaws, and I supposed I did love them for making North and bringing him into my life. For that reason, I didn't disagree.

After ending our call with Southerland, North and I finished our wine and reminisced about the holidays we'd spent together so far.

"I'm looking forward to seeing the kids again tomorrow," North said after we'd retold each other the funny and cute stories from our times with my family over the last three years. Even though we'd both been there, we loved rehashing all the best parts of our lives together. "They're going to be really excited by our surprise extra gift, don't you think?"

"Can't think of a red-blooded boy who wouldn't be thrilled to hear they were getting a pony."

"And Maeve said she'd bring me another one of those sweet potato casseroles I love." North shifted in the blanket, finishing his wine and putting it aside on the small table next to the sofa. I did the same.

"You didn't get your fill today with the four helpings you had?"

"Nope. And Maeve said she didn't mind making it for me."

My sister adored North now that she knew him. She also didn't hate that he was one more person she could hit up for childcare. Especially since Mom had to pick up extra hours at work due to a sick co-worker, and I was still working some of my gig jobs, refusing to give them up entirely until I had the LGBTQ+ Center up and running. I didn't want to be entirely beholden to North's parents.

The first firework of the night rose and burst over the lake. We had the perfect view of it from our deck, and the sparkle of the lights reflected in the water was breathtaking.

North rose to check on Samantha through the glass door into the living room. "She's still asleep. I guess she's too old and deaf to hear it? Sweet girl. I love her."

"I love her, too."

North's smile lit up by the second firework made me feel like crying. I loved *him*. The lump in my throat wouldn't go away. How lucky was I to have this pure-hearted man?

"C'mere," I said, overwhelmed with a sudden need to hold him. I reclined all the way down, and he crawled on to rest beside me. We barely fit. Two grown men on a medium-sized outdoor sofa. But the scent of his hair was reassuring and wonderful, and as the second firework rose, I squeezed him tight, watching it burst in the sky.

Five explosions in, and I whispered, "Watch this one carefully." I hoped Rhonda and Jerome had been able to arrange for the special firework I'd requested.

As the next one shot up, leaving a fire trail in its wake, I waited, delighted when it exploded to reveal Jerome had indeed succeeded at the mission.

North's breath caught. "Look, it's a dragon. How? That's...Liam!"

"I see it," I murmured.

"Wow."

As the dancing lights faded and the dragon dissolved into smoke wafting away on the night air, North turned to me, nearly falling off the sofa as he did, but my arms kept him from disaster.

"You did that, didn't you?"

"Merry Christmas."

North's happy expression made all the effort it'd taken to get such a short-lived present worth it. "I love you, Liam."

"I love you, too. So much. You make me so happy, baby."

"Guess what surprise gift I've got for you?"

"A horse?"

"No."

"A new canoe."

"No. It's incredibly special. One of a kind."

"A—"

"The whole world knows how awesome it is. *Guess.*"

I struggled to think of some popular new item that was all the rage.

North laughed and pressed himself closer to me. Another firework went up. "I'll give you a hint. Some people think it's at the top of the world, but it's really in my pants."

I laughed. "Oh, God."

"It's North's Pole," he whispered in my ear. "Want to unwrap it now?"

"You know I do."

As the finale of the Camp Bay Chalet fireworks show went off in a thunderous volley of booms and a shower of lights in the sky, North went off in my hand. Afterward, his lips stayed pressed to mine, breathing my breath and whimpering. I held his dick until it was soft, and I brought my hand up to lick it clean, tasting his cum.

This, him, us. We were lucky. This life was such a gift.

Cuddling close, swaddled in thick blankets, breathing each other in, and watching the stars reappear as the firework smoke drifted away into the night, I thought about *Hashtag North's Pole* with an unbearable fondness. While I'd have spared North the pain of that humiliation at any cost, I still couldn't help but be thankful for the mishap. It's what brought North home to me, after all.

Petting North's hair and kissing his cheek, I thanked God for him and for our life together. Pure. Loyal. True. The whole world may have seen North's cock, but his love had always been mine alone. And he'd always had my heart. He always would.

I was his hero, and he was my direction—my North Pole, yes, but also my North Star.

"Merry Christmas, Liam," North whispered.

"Merry Christmas, baby."

THE END

Can't let Camp Bay or the characters go?

Check out other Camp Bay universe books:

Want to know more about **Eric and Max**? Pick up Stolen Christmas by Marie Sexton!

Books with Characters Connected to the Camp Bay universe

Want to know more about **Ashton and Walker**? Pick up Mr. Jingle Bells by Leta Blake!

Want to know more about **Haven and Pierce**? Pick The Well by Marie Sexton!

Letter from Leta Blake

Dear Reader,

Thank you so much for reading *North's Pole*! I adored writing the sweet story of Liam and North. It was a sweet, light place to escape to this past year. I hope you loved them, too.

If you enjoyed North and Liam's love, please take a moment to leave a review! Reviews not only help readers determine if a book is for them, but also help a book show up in searches.

The absolute best way to keep up with me is to join my newsletter. I send one out on average once per week. There you'll find all my upcoming news, as well as information on releases.

Also to make sure you never miss a book from me, you can follow my author page at BookBub or Goodreads to be notified whenever there is a new release or deal. To see some sources of my inspiration, you can follow my Pinterest boards. And look for me on Facebook or Instagram for snippets of the day-to-day writing life, or join my Facebook Group for announcements and special giveaways.

For the audiobook connoisseur, many of my books are available in audio, and all are performed by skilled and talented narrators. Look for me on Audible.

Thank you so much for being a reader!
Leta Blake

*In the **Boy for All Seasons** universe*

MY DECEMBER DADDY
by Leta Blake

Matthew Angel is stuck. He's spent his life denying who he is and what he truly wants—until he stumbles upon a unique offering at a specialty charity auction:

A Christmas Daddy experience.

Erik Garner has given up on relationships. After his last boy left, he decided it's better to skip the heartache and stick with casual, short-term contracts. His offer of an exclusive, one-night-only Christmas encounter is all he's willing to give.

Matthew's different from what Erik expected, but his shy smile and eager surrender charm him. What starts out as a business transaction quickly gives way to a wild, thrilling intensity neither expected.

One night isn't enough.

Good thing there's a blizzard on the way...

From the Mr. Christmas series

MR. JINGLE BELLS
by Leta Blake

Opposites attract as frosty business partners become fake boyfriends in this Christmas gay romance!

Playing fake boyfriends starts their sleigh ride into love!

After an emergency forces Ashton Sellers from his apartment, all he wants for Christmas is new lipgloss, zero contact from his abusive family, and a place to stay for the holidays. Cue his business partner begrudgingly taking him in.

Walker's a fuddy-duddy with no sense of fun, but he does have a safe, warm home with four adorable dogs and delicious food on the table.

If it turns out Walker's also a secret softy with a tender side and a hot body beneath his endless parade of golf shirts? Great, good, cool. And if Walker wants Ashton to pretend to be his boyfriend for his sister's Christmas-themed wedding? Awesome, amazing.

Could Walker be the safe haven Ashton missed out on as a child? Could they be falling in love for real?

But when Ashton uncovers a painful mistake in Walker's past, it hits too close to home. As the jingle bells quiet and the snow settles, will Ashton be able to forgive Walker, or will their relationship be over before it ever truly begins?

From the Cherries series

PUNCHING THE V-CARD
by Leta Blake

Best friend's hot older brother? Check. A weekend alone? Check.

Finally punching that V-card? Oh yes.

Carl has a pesky "innocence" problem that requires a solution. His best friend's brother Devon is the perfect answer.

Devon's experienced, gorgeous, and Carl's been secretly crushing on him for ages. Carl doesn't want to "lose it" to just anybody. Everyone says the first time should be special—and what's more special than sharing it with the guy of his dreams?

It's not like Devon won't enjoy it. Solving this so-called problem is an objectively fun experience for most people! The plan is totally win/win!

Shockingly, Devon agrees. But even though it goes better than either of them ever expected, Carl's moving across the country soon. It's not possible to have more. No matter how much they both want it.

Right?

From the Wake Up Married series

WILL & PATRICK WAKE UP MARRIED
EPISODES 1-3

Episode One: Will & Patrick Wake Up Married

After a drunken night of hot sex in Vegas, strangers Will Patterson and Dr. Patrick McCloud wake up married. A quickie divorce is the most obvious way out—unless you're the heir of a staunchly Catholic mafia boss with a draconian position on the sanctity of marriage. Throw their simmering attraction into the mix and all bets are off!

Episode Two: Will & Patrick Meet the Family

Meeting the family is challenging for every new couple. But for Will and Patrick, the awkward family moments only grow more hilarious—and painful—when they must hide the truth of their predicament from the people they care about most. Throw in the sexual tension flaring between them and you've got a recipe for madcap laughs and surprisingly heartwarming feels.

Episode Three: Will & Patrick Do the Holidays

A couple's first holiday season is always a special time. Thanksgiving, Christmas, and New Year's Eve are magical when you're in love. Too bad Will and Patrick's marriage is a sham and they're only faking their affection for each other. Or are they? Sparks fly in this episode of the Wake Up Married serial. Will the sexual tension between Will and Patrick finally explode in a needy night of passion? Or will they continue to deny their feelings?

ANY GIVEN LIFETIME
by Leta Blake

He'll love him in any lifetime.

Neil isn't a ghost, but he feels like one. Reincarnated with all his memories from his prior life, he spent twenty years trapped in a child's body, wanting nothing more than to grow up and reclaim the love of his life.

As an adult, Neil finds there's more than lost time separating them. Joshua has built a beautiful life since Neil's death, and how exactly is Neil supposed to introduce himself? As Joshua's long-dead lover in a new body? Heartbroken and hopeless, Neil takes refuge in his work, developing microscopic robots called nanites that can produce medical miracles.

When Joshua meets a young scientist working on a medical project, his soul senses something his rational mind can't believe. Has Neil truly come back to him after twenty years? And if the impossible is real, can they be together at long last?

Other Books by Leta Blake

Contemporary

Will & Patrick Wake Up Married
Will & Patrick's Endless Honeymoon
Cowboy Seeks Husband
The Difference Between
Bring on Forever
Stay Lucky

Sports

The River Leith

The Training Season Series
Training Season
Training Complex

Musicians

Smoky Mountain Dreams
Vespertine

New Adult

Punching the V-Card

'90s Coming of Age Series
Pictures of You
You Are Not Me

Winter Holidays

North's Pole

The Mr. Christmas Series
Mr. Frosty Pants
Mr. Naughty List
Mr. Jingle Bells

A Boy for All Seasons
My December Daddy

Fantasy

Any Given Lifetime

Re-imagined Fairy Tales

Flight
Levity

Paranormal & Shifters

Angel Undone
Omega Mine

Horror

Raise Up Heart

Omegaverse

Heat of Love Series
Slow Heat
Alpha Heat
Slow Birth
Bitter Heat

For Sale Series
Heat for Sale
Bully for Sale

Audiobooks

Leta Blake at Audible

Discover more about the author online

Leta Blake
letablake.com

Gay Romance Newsletter

Leta's newsletter will keep you up to date on her latest releases, sales and deals, future writing plans, and more from the world of M/M romance. Join Leta's mailing list today.

Leta Blake on Patreon

Become part of Leta Blake's Patreon community to support her indie publishing expenses and to access exclusive content, deleted scenes, extras, and interviews.

About the Author

Author of the bestselling book *Smoky Mountain Dreams* and fan favorites like *Training Season*, *Will & Patrick Wake Up Married*, and *Slow Heat*, Leta Blake has been captivating M/M Romance readers for over a decade. Whether writing contemporary romance or fantasy, she puts her psychology background to use creating complex characters and love stories that feel real. At home in the Southern U.S., Leta works hard at achieving balance between her writing and her family life.